We Need Reviewers

If you enjoy this *Inkception Books* product, please consider writing a review and posting it to any site where *Inkception Books* are sold. This gets the word out about our products. In appreciation for any reviews we receive on this product, you can receive a one dollar rebate on any *Inkception Books* product. Just email inkceptionbooks@gmail.com with a link to the review you gave, and a copy of the receipt for the product you would like the rebate on. Thanks very much for your continued support of our authors!

Call for Submissions

If you are a writer, please submit to *Inkception Books*.

Check out our website at *inkceptionbooks.net* for the latest information about calls for submissions. We publish anthologies of shorts, poems, and we have begun to publish collections of single author works. We would be interested in publishing series of novels as well as stand alone short stories in ebook format. Our next slated projects will include shorts of Science Fiction and shorts for Young Adults. We split royalties on single-author works after cost. Multi-author collections are given rebates on book sales.

Upcoming Releases

DEBORAH K STEEN LPC

LIFE ON THE DEEP END

Living with Chronic Illness

Now Available

Pandora's Box

THE NEW FRONTIER
SHORT FICTION AND POEMS FROM AN OLD AND NEW WORLD

THE CREEPY COLLECTION
FREAKY STORIES FOR CAMPFIRES, STORMY NIGHTS, AND UNDER THE COVERS

SHOWFOLK & Stories
8 PORTRAITS OF PLAYERS ONSTAGE AND OFF

Copyright © 2018 Inkception Books

All rights reserved. No part of this book may be reproduced or transmitted in any form or by any means, electronic, or mechanical, including photocopy, recording, or by any information storage and retrieval system, without permission in writing from the publisher.

This is a work of fiction.

Any resemblance it bears to reality is entirely coincidental.

Love me or hate me,
Both are in my favor.
If you love me I,
I will always be in your heart.
If you hate me,
I will always be in your mind.

William Shakespeare

Sweet Treats

Blondes Prefer Gentlemen ..11
by Michael Osias

Dinner for Two 33
by Angel Rodrigues

Etch--a-- Sketch...................39
by Michael Osias

Forever Seventeen............45
by Michael Osias

Spicy Delights

Runaway Wife 58
by Kay Elam

Prime Time 70
by Kay Elam

Fractured Love Story 96
by Lisa Berryhill

Penelope's Handbag ...113
by Jennifer Steen

Sour After Hours

The Fallen Leaves........124
by Pragya Vishnoi

A Drop Of Memory 131
by Pragya Vishnoi

Good Bye....................143
by Anusha VR

Sweet Treats

blondes prefer gentlemen

by Michael Osias

Sometimes an old picture, a song from years ago, or even a single word can cause memories to resurface. Memories so clear it seems they just happened yesterday. For me, it is a scent, a gentle lingering aroma that never fails to bring me back to that single day, the day I spent with her.

Monday, March 20--1950

Half asleep I crawled out of bed, staggered into the hallway and picked up the receiver of the ringing telephone.

"Hello."

"We have a shoot today and I'll need you."

Inkception Books

Those were the words I'd been waiting to hear since I got hired. I dropped out of school a month before, determined to get a job and a make a few bucks to keep my convertible on the road. Besides the expense of gas and maintenance, I needed to rustle up fifteen dollars a month to cover the payments to my uncle who sold it to me.

I lived for that car, spending hours each day tweaking the engine, washing, waxing and polishing. When I had enough gas, you'd find me in Santa Monica relaxing on the beach, on a sunny afternoon, enjoying the view. I spent the warm early evenings cruising Sunset Boulevard with the top down hoping to meet a nice young lady. Of course, I never did, being too shy I would have panicked, flushing every shade of red if one of those beautiful girls strolling through Hollywood had ever looked my way. Like most seventeen year olds I spent much of my time dreaming about girls, hoping one day a pretty gal would snuggle up close to me and we'd cruise the strip together in the warm night air, not a care in the world. It was a dream and those walking the streets of Hollywood were used to seeing me in my 1940 cloud mist grey Ford, driving back and forth, alone. Some of the reg-

Always and for Never

ulars took to calling me the Lone Ranger and would often shout it out as I drove past for the tenth time in a single evening. They were wrong of course; at least the Lone Ranger had Tonto.

When I answered the ad for a photographer's assistant, I felt sure it would be a waste of time, not having any experience and all but Mr. Clark didn't seem to care.

"You'll learn," he said.

The problem is I hadn't learned a thing or received a single penny in wages. I only got paid when I worked and since my hiring, two weeks had passed without any assignments, until that morning.

"Should I come to the studio? I can leave right now and be there in twenty minutes. Is there anything I need to bring? How should I dress?" I blurted all this out way to fast, failing at my attempt to appear calm and professional.

"Whoa, Lenny. First, don't come to the studio. We are on location, Griffith Park. Make sure you wear clothes or it could prove embarrassing when you pick up the model I'm shooting, supposedly a 'hot tomato'. There's some parking spaces halfway between the merry-go-round and the zoo. We can meet there at eleven."

He told me the address and name of the model and said she'd be expecting me at ten-twenty. That left me plenty of time to get cleaned up and give the Ford a once over, making it shine.

Hoping to impress my new boss I wore my only dress jacket, a maroon, corduroy sport coat, a pair of light grey gabardine slacks, a white shirt and a flamboyant designed silk tie in the same colors of my pants and jacket. I completed the ensemble with a pair of brick sole, ivory white, slightly scuffed Bucks given to me by a cousin who didn't like them any longer.

I worked a glob of Vaseline into my black hair and ran a comb through it creating a slicked back style with a strong part on the left side and a twirl in the front. A final glance in the mirror and I couldn't help but notice a slight resemblance to the movie star, Clark Gable; a much younger, skinnier and less attractive version, of course.

The address given to me -1309 North Harper Avenue in West Hollywood--turned out to be less than twenty minutes from the park. I arrived on time and parked in front of a clean, three story Spanish colonial apartment building, typical of the area. I got out of my car and

Always and for Never

leaned against the trunk attempting to look casual while waiting for the 'hot tomato' to make an appearance.

My inexperience with the fairer sex soon had me perspiring or perhaps I was a little over-dressed for such an unusually warm morning. No, it was the thought of being alone with a pretty model, with any girl, that made me sweaty nervous. I convinced myself to remain professional. This was a job and I should treat it as such.

After ten minutes, I strolled to the front entrance prepared to ring the buzzer but the name on the door wasn't the same as Mr. Clark had given me. I panicked thinking I may have misread or even worse written down the address incorrectly, not very impressive for my first day of employment. While walking back to the car to double check the note where I recorded the instructions I heard the door behind me open, followed by a honey sweet voice.

"Hello, are you here to take me to the shoot?"

I turned around to respond but couldn't, my words disappeared somewhere between the sudden rapid thumping of my heart and my brain which inexplicably stopped working. Somehow I had also forgotten to breathe and the longer I was without air the faster my blood raced seeking the oxygen badly needed to prevent me from fainting. Before me stood the loveliest woman, I had ever seen. She glowed with a light emanating from within, creating an atmosphere of natural and warm beauty that was making me dizzy. I'm not sure how long I basked in her smile before I finally took a much-needed breath and nervously mumbled two words.

"Y-yes, ma'am."

With an exaggerated hurt look matched by a small pout, she softly scolded me, "Do you really think I look that old? I'm barely twenty-four. Surely I don't qualify as a ma'am!"

Straining to concentrate I could feel the wheels in my brain slowly moving again and her name came back to me.

"Of course you don't. Please accept my apologies, Miss Monroe."

"Call me Marilyn," she spoke softly, while extending her hand.

I cannot find a reason or explanation for what I did next. It was very unlike me and something I had never done. Maybe because everything felt unreal, like a dream or perhaps it was the way she held out her hand,

Always and for Never

I'm not sure. Gently taking her fingers in my palm, I bent from the waist and softly kissed her hand, like I had seen in the movies. Realizing what I was doing quickly brought on a wave of anxiety, but she accepted it as the most natural thing in the world and as a result the anxiousness passed and I relaxed. Lingering for a moment my lips still touching her skin I took a deep breath and found myself drifting in her scent; the sweet aroma of freshly picked sun ripened peaches.

"How gallant, surely a dashingly dressed gentleman like you has a name."

"My name is Leonard, Miss Monroe. My friends call me Lenny."

"Pleased to meet you, Lenny. But we can't be friends unless you stop calling me Miss Monroe – Marilyn, please."

"Okay I'll try...Marilyn."

She chuckled lightly and said, "Now we're friends, Lenny."

Unable to move, she stepped around me leading the way to the Ford. I tried not to look at her but couldn't stop myself. Petite yet curvaceous I found her natural sway hypnotizing, again forcing me to concentrate on breathing.

"I can see you take care of your car. Nice and shiny, I like it, Lenny. Does the top go down?"

Beaming from the compliment, I replied "It sure does. Would you like me to lower it?"

"Oh no, not now, can't mess up my hair. I'm sure your boss wouldn't like that. I must be perfect and everything in place for the shoot. Maybe on the way back though. I just love convertibles."

It was then I noticed how she was dressed, and yes everything was in place and fit her perfectly. Her beige collared button down blouse was tight enough to show she was indeed a woman but loose enough to show she was also a lady. A simple monogram, placed slightly below the left collar tip had been neatly stitched with the letters MM, and her snug fitting white cotton shorts showcased her thin waist, round hips and firm, shapely legs. Simple sandals with ankle straps adorned her feet with toenails painted the faintest shade of pink. She toted a white cloth hand bag also displaying her initials, although larger and more decorative.

I opened the passenger door taking her bag as she slipped inside effortlessly.

Always and for Never

"Thank you, Lenny. You are quite courteous. Women admire that, you know?"

Blushing I handed it back to her making a comment about it's weight and a poor joke about what might be inside.

Kindly, she laughed and said, "They're books, poetry books. I love to read."

And off we went. I dared not glance at her for fear of falling under her spell again and perhaps driving off the road, crashing into a tree.

"I'm excited about today," she said.

"You like these photo shoots, do you?"

"It's not the shoot, although I am looking forward to it, Lenny, but today is the first day of spring and it's so beautiful. What better place to be than Griffith Park? My aunt would take me there when I was a little girl and we would have so much fun. The carousel is wonderful; I went on it when it was new. I love the carved wooden horses and their jeweled bridles – colorful and magnificent and each of them a jumper. I would pretend to be a princess galloping through my father's kingdom. Magical, that's the only word for it."

Her soft voice rippled with childlike glee and I

welcomed her enthusiasm. I think it was at this point I began to realize her honest natural beauty came from a special place, much deeper than the eyes could see.

She became very quiet for a time and I thought perhaps she was simply reflecting, lost in thought, but the atmosphere changed within the car and an air of melancholy replaced the joyfulness experienced earlier. I knew it came from her so I looked over and saw her struggle with one lonely tear clinging to a bottom eyelash, refusing to drop. Feeling like an intruder I looked away. Her vulnerability touched me in a way I didn't understand and it pained me to see her in such a state. Like her beauty she couldn't contain her sadness.

Hoping to draw her away from whatever unhappy thoughts may have brought on such a mood I attempted to change the subject.

"Do you enjoy your career as a model, Miss Monroe?"

She hesitated, took a breath, composed herself and replied, "That's not my career. It does pay the rent, keeps me fed and in my favorite red lipstick, but I am primarily an actress."

"An actress? There are so many people trying to

Always and for Never

break into movies. It must be difficult with all the competition?" I didn't know what I was talking about but thought it sounded professional and more importantly it continued to distract her.

"You know something, Lenny – sometimes when I look at the Hollywood night, I think there must be thousands of girls sitting alone like me, dreaming of becoming a movie star. But I'm not going to worry about them. I'm dreaming the hardest."

With such strong conviction in her words I instantly became a believer. Without a doubt, she would be a star.

We arrived a few minutes late and I spotted Mr. Clark standing by the road side with two cameras hanging around his neck and a small leather case strung over his shoulder. I jumped out of the car, dashed around it and opened the passenger door. Miss Monroe took my hand and I helped her out of the seat.

"Lenny, you're spoiling me with all this fine treatment and I'll tell you what I think about it. Good manners and politeness are the mark of a true gentleman and I don't know of anything more appealing to a lady."

She made me feel good and bold; not afraid to

speak the things I practiced, wishing for the opportunity to say to a girl. I surprised myself with my response, "And, you certainly are a fine lady, Miss Monroe."

"Thank you, you are very nice, but aren't you supposed to call me Marilyn?"

"Well if it's all the same to you I'd rather not for now. I don't know my new boss very well and wouldn't want him to think me aggressive or forward. I hope you don't mind."

She looked at me, the sparkle back in her eyes and conspiracy in her hushed voice, "Well when he's not around... Marilyn, okay?"

I replied quietly, "Yes, Marilyn."

Mr. Clarke introduced himself to Marilyn and after a short conversation we slowly began to walk into a forested area near a brook that ran through the park.

My training began while Miss Monroe took a practiced approach to preparing herself, applying make-up and styling her hair. Mr. Clark showed me how to load film without exposing it. He instructed me on how to properly use a light meter and to adjust the setting required for the best photographic result. Giving me an idea on the background he wanted he sent me ahead to

Always and for Never

scout out some suitable spots with the best ambient lighting. I found it all very interesting, not as interesting as Miss Monroe but I was at work and whether I liked it or not, would have to make sacrifices.

The idea of searching locations to take some photos of her seemed unnecessary to me. The city dump could have been the backdrop and no one would have noticed, not with her in the picture. Regardless, I found a wooden bridge and an area where the stream narrowed with plenty of trees and shrubbery, all offering the light Mr. Clark needed.

Returning unnoticed I stood for a while and watched Mr. Clark at work. Marilyn stood by a tree and constantly changed her position, stance and expression. He encouraged and re-assured her with every camera click.

'That's good, look my way, good, now to the side, perfect, the other side, hug the tree, face me again, perfect, a big smile, pout now, very nice," and so on.

Finished, he handed me the camera to load a new roll of film.

"Well, Lenny, how did you make out?"

I let him know what I found; he nodded and indicated that it should be fine.

Mr. Clark took a few moments to instruct Miss Monroe on what he planned to do next. He told her to just be herself, to do whatever she felt.

"Pretend you are alone," he said. "There is no camera, pretend it isn't there. Can you do that, pretend?"

"I have been pretending all my life. That's why I chose to be an actress, I can pretend anything."

Taking a poetry book out of her bag she began to read, slowly strolling down the pathway, then she stopped and lay upon the forest floor softly reciting poems by Carl Sandburg. I was entranced, not sure if it was the poetry or the sound of her delightful voice that captured my attention. The more I listened it became easy to decide, it was her voice, breathless and sexy and I felt she spoke the words just for me.

Mr. Clarke continued to shoot.

At the bridge, she handed me the book, grasped the wooden rail, bent slightly and peered into the brook below, intently. Mesmerized, I could not take my eyes off her. In bare feet she played on the banks of the creek and it thrilled me to see how much she enjoyed it. Somehow her presence in the forest made the first day of spring fin-

Always and for Never

er, more alive. It felt good being around her; she could do that just by being herself. I never knew anyone else like her and never would.

The late afternoon light faded and Mr. Clark, happy with all the candid shots of Marilyn, told her she was a natural and called it a day. He wanted me at the studio the following morning at nine to teach me film developing and darkroom techniques. He hoped we would be able to process all of Miss Monroe's photos and send them on to Life Magazine for approval.

He then handed me a crisp twenty-dollar bill. Seeing the shocked look on my face he smiled and said.

"Eight bucks for today, the rest is for waiting around two weeks. I have more shoots coming up so you'll be getting plenty of work over the next while. Now, how do you feel about driving Marilyn home?"

Before I could say yes sir, Miss Monroe turned to me and asked, "Would you mind staying in the park a little longer. I love it here, Lenny. How about we go for a walk?"

I didn't believe the day would get any better but it did.

"Yes, Miss Monroe, I would be honored to escort

you on a pathway stroll."

We waved goodbye to Mr. Clark and as he drove away he flashed a knowing smile my way.

"He's gone now," she said, "Marilyn, remember."

"Marilyn, it is."

We found a nearby path and walked together, actually that's not the truth; I floated, my feet not touching the ground.

Being nervous I said very little and the peacefulness of a late Monday afternoon drifted with us along the shaded walkway. I learned words were not necessary to communicate and silence a wonderful language, easily shared. And, just as I was having these thoughts, Marilyn said.

"It's often just enough to be with someone. I don't need to touch them. Not even talk. A feeling passes between two people and you know you're not alone."

We arrived at the zoo and she seemed to change, obviously uncomfortable. I couldn't tell why. Perhaps the smell, the condition of the animals or the crowd upset her.

Hesitant to inquire I did what I do best when I don't know what to say; distraction.

Always and for Never

"How about an ice cream cone, Marilyn? My treat." That crisp twenty was burning a big hole in my slacks and I felt an urgent need to get her away from the area.

"Oh yes, I could go for a two scoop."

Heading to the vendor, Marilyn suddenly stopped.

'Look, Lenny a tiny bear cub. One of the staff is bottle feeding the sweet little thing. Let's see if we can pet it."

Sitting on a bench in front of the bear enclosure one of the uniformed employees cradled a tiny cub feeding and baby-talking to it, like anyone would an infant. A small crowd had gathered to watch.

Marilyn could hardly contain her excitement. The little girl behind her deep blue eyes danced and I was happy to see her demeanor change so. As we drew closer she blurted out, "Can I hold it please? It's so cute and cuddly. Only for a minute, please."

The attendant started to mumble something about rules and regulations until he looked at who posed the question. When he did he stood and quickly handed the baby bear over to her. I could easily see when it came to men she had little difficulty getting their attention and cooperation.

"Oh it's so tiny," she cooed, "What a cutie you are. Why is your mama not feeding you?" Raising her eyes to the zoo worker she asked, "Where is she? Where's this little guy's mamma?"

He turned toward the cage and pointed at a large black bear pacing back and forth with odd repetitive motions, "That's her right there, ma'am."

Marilyn looked puzzled and after a short pause, asked, "Why isn't she feeding it? How come the poor thing has been taken from her mother?" Her expression turned to deep concern, "Why would you do that?"

"The mother rejected it, doesn't want it. Sometimes happens in nature. She won't have anything to do with it – wouldn't care if it died."

The same tear that hung on her bottom eyelash earlier re-appeared and this time won the battle followed by others that quickly began to stream down her cheeks. She hugged the little cub tight, warm tears landing on the soft fur. Kissing the tiny nose, she handed it back.

Between heartbreaking, soft sobs she said, "Let's go, Lenny."

Always and for Never

She held my arm and rested her head on my shoulder as we headed back down the path toward the car. It was another silent walk other than her deeply sad crying.

Halfway back she spoke. "That's me, the little cub."

I waited, letting her talk.

"The closest I ever came to having a father was on the merry-go-round pretending. And, my mother didn't want me, she didn't want to have anything to do with me. Like the baby bear, I too was rejected."

I began to speak not sure what I should say but she put her finger to my lips and shushed me.

'It's all right, Lenny. You don't need to say anything; I just wanted you to know. Let's talk about happier things."

By the time we arrived at the car -with my help-- she had shed the gloominess. I felt good about that, making her smile again with a few silly jokes and a poor imitation of a gorilla hanging from a tree branch scratching his belly. She laughed hard and said something I never forgot.

"If you can make a girl laugh, you can make her

do anything."

Reaching for the roof clasps on the car I asked, "Shall I take the top down, Marilyn?"

"Oh yes, and let's go for a fast drive on the highway, Lenny, and let the wind blow away the day."

"Sounds like fun, a nice drive at sunset before I take you home."

We jumped on Ventura highway, the Ford's flathead V8 hummed and had us doing eighty in a blink. The sun seemed to be taking it's time, nestled above the horizon keeping the day warm. Marilyn stood above the windshield allowing the rushing air to fly through her hair. She spread her arms out and threw her head back laughing. When I looked at her; the way the sun caressed her skin creating a golden glow and how it shone as it filtered through her blonde hair, I could see her aura and with her arms extended like wings, I saw an angel in flight and knew no matter how lonely she sometimes felt, at that moment she was truly happy, and so was I. She did that for people, made them happy, just by being.

From Ventura, I hit Hollywood Highway and headed south to Sunset Boulevard. As we were exiting Marilyn sat down and to my delight snuggled up to me.

Always and for Never

"Let's cruise the strip for a while, Lenny. Do you want to?"

As I said earlier, she just knew and I don't know how.

With Marilyn cuddled up nice and close, the Ford purring and the streets busy, we drove the strip for two hours. Plenty of the regulars looked my way but not one called me the Lone Ranger and more than a few gave me an affirmative nod and a most respectful thumbs up.

It was the best night of my young life and I thought nothing could top it except...

I walked her to the door and stumbled awkwardly attempting to tell her how grateful I felt for such a day and all she had done for me.

She placed her hands on each of my cheeks and moved her face so close to mine her enchanting fragrance warmly held me in her spell.

"No, I need to thank you, Lenny. I had a wonderful day, one of the best in a long time. You're a sweet guy but most of all you're a gentleman and there are few of you around. Don't ever change, be yourself because you are an individual and if you let others determine who you are your happiness will be sacrificed. Wanting to be someone else is a waste of the person you are."

Then she kissed me.

I've heard it said by some that if they can touch just one person's life and make it better they are satisfied.

Miss Monroe touched my life and made it better. She gave me confidence, a strong sense of worth and words of advice that I have kept with me all my life. I never drove the strip alone after that day.

Her lips were soft, they were moist and when she parted them slightly and tickled me with her wet tongue, I went crazy for a moment. It was a woman's kiss, an honest kiss, hungry and lingering, more than I had known or imagined--I became light headed. It wasn't my first kiss but made me forget those before and the best thing about it; a soft sound she made, a moan, saying she was enjoying it as much as I.

Marilyn's kiss will stay with me forever because with it came something special, something that transports me back to that single incredible day, something that will always belong to her and to me--the delicate scent of fresh picked, sun ripened peaches.

dinner for two

by Angel Rodriguez

Dolores was an old-fashioned kind of woman and dating at her age was unheard of. She had been taught proper manners and etiquette. Laying your napkin across your lap while eating, and dabbing the corner of one's mouth after each bite. Tonight however, Dolores was not thinking about her manners or the proper placement of her silverware, even though she did manage to lay her linen napkin across her lap once she sat down. Tonight all Dolores could think about was the betrayal she was committing and so soon after her husband's death.

"It hasn't been very long since Henry died, I should just leave now. This just isn't right," she thought.

Inkception Books

Fraught with guilt, Dolores could hardly enjoy even the most tender of morsels of roast beef. Reaching for each bite, Dolores's aged, yet elegant hand grasped her fork, trembling and, shaking each piece free from the prongs. The struggle left her with only one thought, "Henry loved roast beef," she sighed. "Why did I ever accept such an invitation when I am still married to my Henry? Till death, do us part but there is no one who will replace my beloved Henry. I can never part."

Henry was such a sweet man. She remembered the two of them sitting down at Christmas watching the tree all lit up, each branch carefully wrapped with bulbs, just the way he liked it. He always turned and told her she was beautiful during moments like these. Henry knew Dolores like the back of his hand and always bought her the best presents for every holiday.

One year Dolores opened her Valentine's Day candy heart box with the velvet cover and ribbon around it to find Henry had managed to slide in tickets to a Broadway show of Hello Dolly. She still cannot figure out how he did that without disturbing the wrap around the box. Henry also knew that every year on the fourth of July she had to get sparklers to celebrate the Indepen-

Always and for Never

dence of the country Henry had fought so hard to protect in his youth and even in his last years he made sure the postman delivered her a bouquet of sparkers with her mail that day. He tipped the man twenty dollars just to make sure it went off without a hitch.

Dolores's beliefs in tradition were so sewn into the fabric of her being that she couldn't shake the feeling that she was committing some grand grand mortal sin today by dining with another man. "He's nice and all, but my Henry and I were married forty-two years and no other man could take his place."

Henry had been a hardworking man his whole life, but he developed heart problems, maybe something from the war. Financially Henry and Dolores never wanted for anything that Henry couldn't provide. Even if it meant a bowl of soup and a movie on television, the two couldn't have been any happier. The two of them were not void of troubles that life can sometimes throw at anybody of any means, but Dolores always had a way of making lemons out of lemonade. That's what Henry loved the most about Dolores. When he died, a piece of Dolores went with him. She was never the same again.

"I just can't do this anymore, sir. I'm so sorry, but

I'm going to have to excuse myself and go home," Dolores declared to her dinner companion. "I just don't think I can continue with this dinner, not today, not ever. I am truly sorry, I only want my Henry," she began to quiver with tears as she spoke. Dolores rose from her chair, her crisp white linen napkin slipping to the floor. Red faced from embarrassment because a lady is always a lady regardless of the situation and must never forget her etiquette, she leaned down to pick it up.

"Pardon me; I must go now. Please do not think ill of me and please let me pay for my meal," remarked Delores as she picked up the napkin.

"But Dolores, I am right here," her dinner companion said. Dolores slowly raised her head, napkin in her hand, her breath labored and heart racing. Dolores stood at the dinner table and the man she saw before her had gone. Like a magician's trick, a slight of hand card ruse, Dolores thought her eyes were playing tricks on her. The man was gone, but yet there remained another male figure. There he was, looking almost familiar yet unrecognizable.

Dolores blinked frantically trying to adjust her mind to what was going on. Befallen with anxiety and

Always and for Never

confusion, she took herself to her seat again at the table. The man continued to speak and as he did her eyes came into focus. "See my darling; I would never leave you. I knew you were not ready to see me. The shock would be too great, so I came to you as a stranger, forgetting how traditional you are and how you would never stay for the meal. Please finish your roast beef. It's your favorite. Dolores thought she must have banged her head on the table picking up her napkin and now she was seeing things. Hearing things. It was her Henry.

"Could it really be you Henry?" she gasped.

"Not only is it me my dear Dolores, but I am never leaving you again, for it is true that you do get to spend eternity with those that you love in heaven," he replied. We will never be apart again. Not now, not ever," Henry declared.

"I'm dead?" asked Dolores.

"Yes, my dear. Remember the day I passed and you kissed my lips goodbye?" asked Henry.

"I could never forget. I will never forget. Wait, how did you know I kissed you after you passed?" asked Dolores.

"Well, sweetheart that was your last drawn

breath, because just as your lips kissed mine and relaxed, so did your heart. We died seconds apart from each other and now we can spend eternity in each other's arms," said Henry.

"It just took the heavens time to find us the perfect roast beef dinner to celebrate our second life together," proclaimed Henry. The two of them sat for a moment staring at each other, thinking about what it all meant. Henry waiting for Dolores to accept her passing and Dolores waiting to see if this was all real or her imagination running away with her.

Dolores removed herself from the side of the table just as she had done earlier, but this time to run to Henry's open arms. Henry smiled, looked into Dolores's eyes and said, "Our hearts may have once been broken, but now our hearts are whole. Just like that velvet candy box I once gave you, I will continue to surprise you for the rest of eternity."

etch-a-sketch

by Michael Osais

The first time I saw her she was staring at me from the second story window of her grandparents' house. Sitting on my front porch attempting to create a masterpiece maneuvering the knobs of my Etch-a-Sketch I pretended not to notice her. It didn't work because when I looked up, she smiled at me and I couldn't help myself, I smiled back. I didn't usually acknowledge girls and certainly never played with them. Being a member of the ten-year-old 'Boys Only-No Girls Allowed' club, I strictly adhered to the number one rule. Yet, something about her seemed different, kind of special. Her smile made me smile and it felt kind of nice.

For my last birthday, my parents gave me the

Etch-a-Sketch I held in my hands that day.

For those of you who don't know, let me explain how it works. It's a drawing toy with a small gray screen about ten inches square and has two knobs on the front in the lower corners. Twist the knobs and lines appear on the screen, left knob horizontal and right vertical. Turn the screen over, give it a shake and you have a blank screen to begin again.

Sounds easy doesn't it? I was crappy at it; everything I drew resembled a mountain range or a weird scientific graph of some kind. It looked a lot easier on TV.

She waved at me and I enthusiastically waved back, beckoning her to come join me. Don't know why I did that, just did. Maybe because she looked so pretty and like I said earlier, special.

I thought I might have scared her because she quickly ran away.

A few minutes later she stepped out the front door holding her grandfather's hand. He called me over.

"Jake, this is Rebecca," he said. "For some reason she insisted I take her out here so she could play with you. First off, you should know, Rebecca can't talk and she can't hear. She has her own way of communicating,

Always and for Never

makes it up as she goes along. Pay attention to her and you might catch on. She's a good teacher and a smart cookie. Be nice to her or I'll kick your ass, ya hear?"

What had I got myself into?

Rebecca followed me back to my porch and when I sat down she sat right beside me. I must admit I never really spoke to a girl on a friendly basis before and I tried to convince myself of the fact she couldn't hear, made it easier. It didn't work. I was so nervous, I shook. She was the most beautiful girl I had ever seen or been this close to and she smelled like fresh picked wild blueberries, my favorite.

We both looked around at nothing much and just sat there for a while. Did I mention that girls make me nervous?

I was relieved when she pointed to my Etch-a-Sketch and indicated she wanted to try it. It gave me something to do. I taught her how it worked and she caught on right away.

Rebecca made me look like a novice. She was a natural, spinning those dials expertly and quickly, creating crazy faces and scenes. We both giggled at each one. Her infectious laughter was the only sound she made and

I loved it.

Finally, she stopped. On the screen, I saw a caricature of a confused looking goofy kid with a pointy head and cowlick just like mine in the middle of his forward. Beads of sweat dripping everywhere from the face.

There was something familiar about it, but I couldn't decide what it might be.

Before I could figure it out she flipped it over and erased it, but she wasn't finished. Twirling the dials, she created letters and turned them into words. Satisfied, she showed me what she wrote.

"That was you. Relax, I promise I won't bite you."

The two weeks she spent at her grandparents were the best of my young life. Together every day, we climbed trees, stealing apples from Mr. Garrets' orchard. Screaming we jumped from what became our favorite rock and swam in the cool water of the creek behind my house. We played nicky-nicky nine doors, hiding in the bushes suppressing our laughter as unsuspecting neighbors answered their doors to no one. We conversed through pantomime and fell down laughing at some of our silliness when we did.

Always and for Never

One evening in her room, she showed me how to do the twist as Chubby Checker encouraged us from a forty-five spinning on her little pink record player. She was a much better twister than I. After Chubby she put on Blue Velvet by Bobby Vinton and we awkwardly slow danced to it ten times in a row. I thought about kissing her that night but didn't know how to make the move.

On her last day, we walked to the creek holding hands. Sitting on our rock we watched the water bubble, carrying twigs and leafs downstream. The occasional trout flashed rainbow colors at us.

I was sad she had to go and she sensed it.

Rebecca took the Etch-a-Sketch out of my pack and began to spin the knobs, hiding her drawing from me. I could see she was enjoying her secret. Between frowns of deep concentration, a smile pulled at the corner of her lips. I tried to steal a peek, but she turned to face me directly keeping the screen from my view.

When finished she held it to her chest and I could tell she was debating about showing it to me.

I nudged her indicating I wanted to see it. She hesitated slightly and then suddenly held it out in front of my face. She had sketched a perfect set of puckering lips and below it she wrote, "Kiss me, I know you want to and I promise I won't bite you."

So, I did and when our lips touched I tasted wild blueberries, my favorite.

forever seventeen

by Michael Osais

They were sixteen when they met.

It was a different time. The Second World War only a few short years passed. Many married young then. The horrors and threats behind them. Cautious optimism and the hope of a brighter future was the order of the day. The beginning of the baby boom. Those who believed in reincarnation, felt that all of these new babies were the returning souls of those who perished on the battlefields. Everyone sensed the time was right begin or resume their lives, stalled by war. The guillotine hanging over their young lives was slowly rusting. Love was eager, love was rushed, and it aided in masking their fear that all the chaos would return. That's the way it was.

They cherished their time together. Spending hours at the local restaurant where she worked. Planning their lives, laughing at silly jokes, whispering soft sweet endearments to each other, and talking late into the night. Happiness was the language they spoke. Dreams of children and growing old together melded their young hearts into one.

It was a time before rock and roll. People danced and listened to Frankie Laine, Bing Crosby, and the Andrews Sisters. They went to the movies to laugh, to see Abbott and Costello acting silly with their zany slapstick antics. Laughter helped to dry the tears of war that were still burning upon their cheeks. The tears they shed for loved ones lost forever.

He took her to the movies, they held hands and shared chuckles at the craziness on the screen. When they went dancing she held him so close that she could feel his heartbeat. She felt safe and secure in his strong arms. They went to the lake to picnic. He taught her how to fish. She cringed and felt sad for the live bait that he put on the sharp hook. When she caught her first fish she giggled and jumped up and down with the pure honest ex-

Always and for Never

citement that it brought to her. And, although he thought it not possible, he loved her even more.

Televisions replaced the shrines once occupied by radios in the living rooms of homes. Housewives followed the soaps and families gathered to watch 'The Adventures of the Lone Ranger'. The memory of the war was drifting away, evaporating like the early morning dew on a sunny day. It was what the people needed, to forget, and to begin again.

She looked into his beautiful eyes and felt them the softest blue she had ever seen. Bluer than the sky, bluer than heaven. She thought of the future, their life together, and the warmth she felt inside made her cry. He asked her to be his forever. He saved his money since the day they met for the modest ring that he placed upon her finger. And, although she thought it not possible, she loved him even more.

They were seventeen.

Youth were now called teenagers. Hawaiian shirts were introduced while the girls wore oversized skirts. The swell thing to wear on your feet were saddle shoes. Frankie, Bing, and the Andrews Sisters made way for Sinatra, Duke Ellington, and Louis Armstrong. Informal dances, sock hops, were held in high school gyms. They danced the jitterbug. People were beginning to find happiness again and joy finally replaced their sadness.

He hated to leave her after each weekend but his work in the remote forest camp left him no choice. And, at the end of each weekend she hated to see him go. They made a promise to one another that every night at the same time they would whisper 'I Love You' to the stars. The same stars that they could both see.

Walking through the forest to the job site that morning it was as if he was seeing everything for the first time. The crisp spring morning sun bounced and glittered off of the trees. A doe with her fawn came so close he almost touched them and the birds flew around him. He held out his hand thinking one might land upon it. The crystal clear brook that hugged his path was singing a love song that he never before noticed.

He arrived at the site and began to drill into the rock. Holes to slip in the dynamite that would blast the rock away so the hydro power towers could be assembled upon flat ground.

Then his world stopped.

The newspaper ran the story about a local boy

Always and for Never

who was injured while working in the bush. He had stood in the midst of a dynamite explosion. Twelve charges had ignited prematurely causing severe injuries. After the slow process of getting him out and to the hospital the outlook was grim. He had been moved to the city and specialists were working around the clock to save his young life.

She sat beside his bed every day and every night. Willing him to live. Never allowing herself to think it was over. She cried herself to sleep each night holding his hand. She held it with her left hand, the one that wore the ring he had given to her. The doctors told her to be prepared for the worst. He would not make it. She never believed them for a moment. She knew that their love was stronger than anything, stronger than dynamite. They told her that if by some slim chance he should live he would be blind. His eyes were lost in the explosion. She thought about those eyes, eyes bluer than heaven and knew that whatever happened she would never forget them. They weren't gone but locked in her heart forever.

The local newspaper ran a follow-up story about a boy who against tremendous odds had returned to his home town. Although blinded he had survived a horrific accident and was to marry the girl that stood by him.

Inkception Books

After raising five children and sixty years of marriage he was once interviewed by a local television reporter who asked him how he managed to accomplish all that he had. He told them that he would never have been able to do it without her by his side.

She never thought him any less or different than the boy she first met and fallen in love with.

And, when he thought of her and how beautiful she looked the last time he saw her, she would be forever seventeen.

Spicy Delights

Runaway Wife

by Kay Elam

Natalie Powell backed her maroon minivan down the steep drive of her suburban Nashville home. It narrowly missed the oversized Rubbermaid trashcan that hugged the curb, filled to the brim with the week's garbage.

"Almost got it, Mom," Bret said from the back seat.

"Yeah, Mom, why don't you go for two outta three?" added Blake.

When Natalie scowled over her right shoulder, the twins high-fived as they laughed. Her cheeks reddened, and she pressed the stereo knob. A little light jazz would calm her down. But what she got was Oscar from

Always and for Never

Sesame Street singing I Love Trash and two kids laughing hysterically.

"Very funny," she said as she popped the CD out of the player and tossed it to the back seat. "I thought you'd outgrown Sesame Street."

The whole garbage can debacle had begun a month earlier when her husband, Kirk, and the boys had come up with the bright idea to fill a Rubbermaid trashcan with forty gifts for her fortieth birthday. She didn't hold the boys responsible for such a hair-brained idea— they were only nine, after all—but Kirk had more sense than that...or so she thought.

Get over it, she told herself. Sunlight danced off the ruby bracelet on her left wrist, by far the best gift of the lot, and she shook her head. She just couldn't get past the fact that even it had been a part of the garbage.

When Kirk had tried to explain the purpose of the trashcan was to protect her car, he'd only made matters worse. Okay, so I hit those old tin cans occasionally...if he'd put them on his side of the driveway like I've begged, he could protect the car, have nice curb appeal, and stay out of hot water with me. Simple. Four weeks had passed, and the incident still infuriated her.

They stopped in front of a house on the next block; she tapped her horn and Jonathan Lewis raced to the car. Jonathan's mom, Sarah, was Natalie's best friend.

The three boys spent the ten-minute ride to school comparing their tennis shoes. It was beyond her comprehension how they could argue over whose shoes were best when there wasn't a pair in the car that cost less than a hundred dollars. Except hers, of course. If she didn't get away from all of this soon, she was going to lose her mind. That's not a bad idea, she thought. I'll run away from home.

Natalie was almost in a good mood when she got home. Her mother-in-law, Edna, was at the breakfast table, sipping black coffee and reading the morning newspaper. The dishwasher hummed in the background and the freshly mopped floor gleamed.

"Edna, how many times have I asked you not to clean when I'm not here? I only ran out to take the boys to school and would've done this as soon as I got home." It's my frickin' house. Why am I justifying my cleaning habits to my mother-in-law?

"I know, honey, but I didn't want any bacteria to set up—you know it doesn't take long for that to happen,

Always and for Never

and that could make the whole family sick."

"I don't think anyone has ever gotten sick from bacteria in my kitchen, Edna." From my cooking, maybe, but not from bacteria.

"Oh, sweetie, I didn't mind. Why don't you sit down and relax? Have another cup of coffee. Want some of the paper?"

I didn't ask you if you minded doing it. I asked you, for about the thousandth time, not to do it. "No thanks. I'm just going to get ready for the day."

Natalie ran a hot bath, pouring in a variety of bath salts. One was to make her relax, one was for sore muscles, and one was supposed to stimulate the thought process. She grabbed her iPod and headphones and lit all of the tranquility candles she could find. After pinning her thick raven hair on top of her head, she slid into the bubbles that swelled in the deep garden tub. Her aching neck rested on a shell-shaped bath pillow while she closed her eyes.

"Calgon, take me away," she said aloud as she rekindled her daydream about running away from home. Money wouldn't be a problem as she still had her inheritance from her parents' unexpected deaths from a wreck ten years ago when on their way to a party announcing her pregnancy. She felt guilty they'd died. Spending any of this money would've been admitting they were really gone, so she'd ignored it for almost a decade, hoping it'd go away and her parents would come back. Of course, the money was still there, and her parents were still dead. She knew it was past time to let go of that fantasy. Maybe she should spend the money, or at least the interest it had earned, to help salvage her sanity.

Natalie closed her eyes and thought about logistics. Of course she couldn't, wouldn't, leave forever—just long enough for her family to miss her and maybe, just maybe, appreciate her. A month seemed like the right amount of time. She could go to the beach. She'd never seen the beach during the winter. She envisioned long walks on the deserted sand, reading the backlog of books stashed beside her bed, and perhaps squeezing in a massage or two. Beach properties were listed in the Sunday vacation section of the paper so she wouldn't need to use her computer to find a place. Kirk was a computer whiz and could find her in no time.

She'd take her cell phone, but not turn it on because of the GPS. She could always buy a disposable

Always and for Never

phone to check in and use locally. She'd tell her best friend, Sarah, how to reach her in case of a real emergency. Sarah loved adventures, and she was trustworthy. Natalie would swear her to secrecy.

By the time she dressed in navy cords and a red and blue striped sweater, Natalie had convinced herself to seriously consider an idea that, before her bath, had simply been a daydream. She had a bounce in her step when she went back to the kitchen and found Edna putting away the dishes, still warm from the dry cycle. Whatever.

She plundered through the junk drawer until she found two pads of sticky notes—one yellow, one blue—and a mechanical pencil. After grabbing a Diet Coke from the refrigerator, she drifted into the den and settled into a comfy recliner in front of the large gas fireplace.

On individual yellow notes, she listed her "pros" for retreat—"cons" on the blue ones—and stuck them on the back of a Good Housekeeping magazine. She realized she'd have to use cash. No credit cards—too easy to trace. She wanted to return home based on her feelings, not on being tracked down like a wounded bear. Her family might miss her—she hoped they would—but that was part of her need to do this. When she finally paused and looked at her collage of sticky notes, it looked like a giant canary with a blue eye. Holy moly, I can actually do this!

The rest of the day was routine—she played Bridge for two hours and then shopped for groceries before picking the kids up from school. The boys were restless; she had to threaten to take away their TV privileges to get them to do their homework. After dinner, they fought over what to watch during prime time as Kirk snoozed behind the newspaper. She kissed them all goodnight and went to bed to read until Kirk joined her.

Natalie tossed and turned all night. By morning, she'd convinced herself her plan was not only irresponsible but also absurd.

At breakfast she reminded Kirk of their date night to the ballet, but he responded with his I don't know what you're talking about stare. He'd made plans to play basketball. She distinctly remembered telling him she'd been given the tickets. True, he'd had his nose buried in The Wall Street Journal as usual, but he was a computer programmer, for goodness sake. The man knew how to multi-task. Besides, he never missed anything his mother told him—no matter how many distractions were around. The trip was on!

Always and for Never

Her mother-in-law had moved in nine years earlier when the twins were born. Recently retired from teaching home economics, everyone had thought this would be a smart move for all. Kirk, like Natalie, was an only child. His father had disappeared on a sailboat when Kirk was only three. Natalie didn't know much about it. Kirk couldn't remember him, and Edna refused to discuss the subject.

Her mother-in-law had sold her house and used some of the money to convert Natalie and Kirk's basement into a lovely apartment, including a full kitchen. In fact, the basement, in Natalie's opinion, was nicer than the rest of the house. But why wouldn't it be? Edna was never there, except to sleep or to retreat when the boys were exceptionally rowdy. She was always upstairs helping Natalie.

Natalie loved Edna and appreciated her help—really she did—but she needed some alone time. Kirk couldn't, or wouldn't, understand her feelings about his mother. Natalie knew they could never ask her to move, especially since she'd paid for the renovations to the basement. It had seemed like such a good idea—at the time. Truth be told, Natalie wasn't sure she could've managed the twins so soon after her parents' deaths without Edna's help, but she was positive she could manage fine now.

Natalie called Sarah and told her to put on coffee. It wasn't uncommon for Natalie to return to her friend's house for a long chat after she'd dropped the boys at school. By the time she walked into Sarah's oversized kitchen, her friend had brewed a pot of an aromatic Kona blend and taken her signature sour cream pound cake from the oven.

"So, you don't think I'm crazy?" Natalie asked, licking the last crumb from her fork. "I mean is this a mid-life crisis or something?"

"So what if it is?" Sarah said. "Edna's there. They'll be fine. You need a break. It's not like you're running off to Mexico with the pool boy."

Natalie laughed. "Yeah, our imaginary pool that Kirk keeps putting off, saying we'll put one in 'next summer.'"

Sarah went to her recycling bin and rummaged through it until she found the Classified Ads from the previous Sunday's Tennessean. "You sure you don't want to go online? It'd be a lot easier."

Natalie flipped open the newspaper and studied

Always and for Never

it. "You're right. There's nothing here."

Sarah turned on her MAC and pulled up VRBO —Vacation Rentals by Owner.

"Is this safe?" Natalie asked.

"It's how I rented the place condo for Jonathan and me when we went to Disney World last summer. I've known several people who've used it. It'll be fine."

"I don't know where to begin.," Natalie said. "It's overwhelming."

Sarah nodded. "I know. First things first. Decide on a location."

"I was thinking the Florida Panhandle.," Natalie said. "Since I'm driving, that's not too far. I could get back in less than eight hours, depending where I went, if there were an emergency,"

"It'll be warmer farther south," Sarah said.

"I know. But there will be lots of people on the beaches where it's warm. I sort of like the idea of walking on a beach with fewer people around."

"Well, if you go with the Panama City side of the panhandle, there will be college kids, lots of college kids, if you overlap with any of their spring breaks."

"What about Pensacola?" Natalie asked.

Sarah sprang from her chair. "I know just the place—be right back," she said as she ran from the room. She returned with a scrapbook and flipped the pages until she found some photos of a much younger Sarah with several girls on a beach.

"These were taken at Gulf Shores."

"In Alabama?" asked Natalie.

"It's still the Gulf of Mexico. Alabama beaches are just as pretty as the Florida ones. I'd look there or nearby at Orange Beach. It's beautiful in that area. If you have to have Florida, If your heart is set on Florida, Perido Key in is just across the state line toward Pensacola."

"I wish you could come with me." Natalie touched her friend's arm.

"Me too, but my alimony runs out next year, so I've got to start getting my resume out there for a teaching job in the fall. I'm finally up to date with my continuing ed."

They pored over the listings, evaluating each one as they drank their coffee and continued to chat.

"Hey, look at this one," Natalie said. "This might be it. 'Orange Beach, Alabama, 1 BDR, condo on 14th floor. Oceanfront. Indoor/outdoor pools, sauna, exercise

Always and for Never

room, full amenities.' What do you think?"

"I think you need to book it before someone else snags it," Sarah said.

"I can't book it online. They'll want a credit card."

"You can use mine and pay me back."

"Thanks, that means a lot...really, but I'll just call and figure out how to book it with cash."

Sarah handed Natalie the phone.

She reserved the unit for a month starting the following Monday. She promised to send a deposit by the end of the day.

"How're you gonna do this so Kirk doesn't know?"

"I've got to wire the money. My bank could do it, but they know me there...and they know Kirk. Do you know where Western Union is?"

"No idea, but we can Google it."

Natalie hugged Sarah liked she was leaving for a year, not a month.

"You can't go if you don't leave," Sarah said, taking a deep breath when released from the embrace by her friend.

Natalie choked back a sob. "I don't know whether I'm happy or sad. I guess I've got a month to figure it out. I couldn't have done it without your support."

"Oh, great," Sarah said. "Kirk already thinks I'm a bad influence. Now he'll really hate me."

Natalie laughed. "He doesn't hate you. He thinks I envy your freedom, and I guess I do. But this was all my doing. You won't be guilty by association. I promise."

When Natalie started to give Sarah yet another hug, Sarah tapped her watch and they both laughed. Natalie left to withdraw enough money for the whole trip and to wire the payment to the property owner. She felt better than she had in months.

~

Natalie had never wired money before. The Western Union office was dark, damp and dirty. The clerk was behind a window with bars, and a yellowish mutt was spread out on the floor slept in front of a noisy space heater. There were a couple of people in line ahead of her. Her heart raced as she thought about where she was and what she was doing. On the other hand, it added to

Always and for Never

the intrigue. When it was her turn, she handed the money to the clerk, a tall, wiry man, and waited for confirmation. It's too late to back out now.

Natalie returned home and made a list. I don't have to worry about the house or meals being cared for, thanks to Edna...She'll be in hog heaven. But, bills must be paid, and Kirk doesn't have a clue how I do them. She prepaid everything she could, and made a list of things that would come due during her absence. She left it under the checkbook on her desk, positive no one would find it until it was needed. She'd moved her desk to a small attic alcove a couple of years earlier. It was heated and cooled, but not much more. The boys and Kirk never went up there, and Edna didn't like to climb the steep, narrow stairs. The tiny space had become Natalie's sanctuary.

She arranged for Merry Maids to come in once a week, even though she knew Edna wouldn't let them do anything. It was the principle of the thing. She considered having food delivered, but decided that would be going too far. She set up a laundry service to pick up and deliver Kirk's shirts twice a week—she'd been meaning to do that anyway—and made a list of important numbers like the plumber, doctors, dentist, etc. She listed the boys' schedules on a calendar and made a list of other things on a yellow legal pad.

Because she didn't want to feel like a wife and mom while she was gone, Natalie decided to take Kirk's Lexus IS C and secured its availability by volunteering to have it serviced the following week. He can drive the Mommy minivan for a change. Just the thought of that made her smile.

She began to feel guilty, so she visited her priest on Friday, three days before her departure. No matter what her arguments, he wouldn't absolve her sins in advance. He advised her to tell Kirk she was leaving town so he wouldn't worry. Father Samuel offered to counsel her and Kirk, or even the whole family. But she was adamant she only needed to get away.

The visit hadn't turned out how she'd planned. *I hope I didn't mess up by talking to Father Sam. No, he won't call Kirk and it won't occur to Kirk to call him. Heck, with me gone, he and the boys will probably take the month off from Mass.*

During the next few days, when no one was home, Natalie snuck luggage to the attic. It made packing easy since she stored her lighter-weight clothes there. She

Always and for Never

took underwear, toiletries, and other items upstairs with her each time she went to her desk.

She put everything she'd need in the trunk of the Lexus on Sunday afternoon. Kirk's mom had taken the boys to the latest Disney movie and dropped Kirk at the YMCA for his weekly basketball game.

Natalie curled up in front of the fire and wrote a note to her husband and each of her sons. She explained to Kirk that Sarah could reach her in an emergency, but asked that he respect her privacy and not ask Sarah to contact her unless it was a legitimate crisis. She told the boys how much she loved being their mom and tried to explain why she felt she had to go away for a while. Writing the notes was cathartic. She even wrote one to Edna. She thanked her mother-in-law for all she'd done since moving in with them and gently suggested she might now want to live her life for herself, not for them.

Natalie considered leaving the notes with Sarah, not to be retrieved until someone actually noticed she was gone, but decided that would be cruel. I'm not cruel. She put Kirk's note with his sweats, which he'd change into as soon as he got home from work on Monday. She mailed the notes for the boys and Edna so they'd have them by

Tuesday. This way she'd have at least an eight-hour head start before she was missed.

Monday dawned to three inches of fluffy snow, but Natalie was undaunted. She got the boys ready for school and reminded Kirk they were switching cars for the day. She had fleeting second thoughts when he volunteered to drop the twins at school so she could wait until the roads were cleared before she headed to the dealership. She'd looked forward to that car time with the boys because she wanted some time alone with them, but decided this would probably be easier for everyone.

She kissed her guys goodbye and told Edna she was going to the dealership for the Lexus's tune-up. She said not to expect her before evening and knew Edna would assume she would be using the Lexus dealer's limousine service to go shopping.

Natalie backed the Lexus out of the drive and ran right over the Rubbermaid trashcan, which—wouldn't you know it—Kirk had put out on his side of the drive.

She didn't stop to assess the damage—to the can or to the car. "Too little, too late," she said as she popped a Beach Boys CD into the player and began singing along

Always and for Never

with them: "Drive, drive, drive, till my Hubby takes his Lexus away!"

prime time

by Kay Elam

Carolyn McAllister stared at the flame of the candle as it melted on the mirror in the middle of the table. Tears pooled in her hazel eyes, but she'd be damned before she'd shed them. She was tired. Tired of the arguments. Tired of his accusations. Tired of his shit. She could hardly wait until he left town the following day. Except then, then she knew she'd miss him. She always did.

"Sorry about that," Steve McAllister, Carolyn's husband of almost thirty 'years said as he scraped his chair on the black and white tiled floor. "It was the network. They have a great new concept for a reality show. I had to take the call."

Always and for Never

"Of course you did." She sipped her Merlot, the last from the bottle they'd ordered. "You always do."

"You could come with me," he said. "It'd be like the early years, before the kids."

"I have a career."

"You have a hobby."

"I'm an interior designer," she said with a sigh. "I didn't work while the kids were at home, but it's my turn now. This is important to me. I've already got some potential clients."

"It sounds to me like an excuse to be alone with men in their homes."

I'm not going there again. Not here. Not now. Get the check."

Heads turned as they walked from the restaurant. Steve, at fifty-five, was just under six feet tall with salt and pepper colored hair and sky blue eyes. His dark suit was tailor made and he wore it well. Carolyn, two years younger, had on a fitted yellow sheath so simple it seemed elaborate. Shoulders back, head high, one would never know her heart was breaking.

~

Inkception Books

Carolyn got busy building her business while Steve was on location during the next three months. Her husband had always made more than enough money for them to have a comfortable lifestyle, but it felt great to earn her own paycheck for a change. She hadn't worked since their first child was born, and he'd be twenty-eight in a few weeks.

Although they talked or used Skype daily, the calls usually ended with Steve accusing her of being unfaithful. She'd never been unfaithful—never even thought about it. But, he'd dreamed a year or so earlier she had cheated on him. Ever since he was convinced she was guilty. They'd talked to a couple's therapist who told Steve it was a dream, not real, but her husband was relentless. It didn't help that three couples from their country club had divorced since his dream. In all three cases, supposedly the wife had had an affair.

Carolyn considered briefly that perhaps Steve was seeing someone and using his accusations as a way to assuage his own guilt. But she dismissed this theory. She wouldn't lower herself to his standards.

Steve agreed to both individual and couples ther-

Always and for Never

apy after this reality series was finished. It was a truce Carolyn could live with. When the first-class ticket to Tahiti arrived via messenger, she rearranged her schedule to join him for the final days of taping followed by a vacation on a private island. Maybe things were turning around.

He met her plane with champagne and roses. His floral print shirt accented the tan he'd acquired during the weeks he'd spent in the South Pacific. He looked good...real good.

"Oh, baby, I've missed you." He picked her up and spun her around. She laughed as her long red hair danced in the breeze.

"I've missed you too, sweetheart. I can't wait to hear all about the show. You've been so elusive about it."

"Until it's finished and we start the promotions, everyone involved—staff, actors, contractors—signed confidentiality agreements," he said.

"And that extends to your wife," she teased. She didn't really care. He usually told her endless stories about his projects when they were finished.

Steve's demeanor changed. "It applies to everyone. This is the network's turn-around-show. If it leaks—

well, it can't. After we'd got on location, we didn't even report back to the network by phone or e-mail due to security issues. One of us flew back each Monday with our update."

After she got her bags, he took her to a private jetway instead of the parking lot.

"Steve, what's going on?"

"We've got another couple of days of shooting before I can get away." He leaned over and kissed her forehead. "I've booked us a bungalow on a private island a short plane ride from here. I'm going to send you on ahead. I'll get there as soon as I can."

She smiled. "Your loss. It'll give me a chance to catch up on my tan."

He laughed and seemed to relax.

"Mike," he said and raised his hand. The most handsome man Carolyn had ever seen walked over and picked up her bags.

"Mike, this is my wife, Carolyn. Honey, Mike is one of our charter pilots. He's taking this company jet back to LA and will drop you at the island."

"Do I get a parachute?"

"I think I can manage a short stop," the pilot

Always and for Never

said. "There's a dirt runway."

"He'll make sure you're settled and have everything you need," Steve said.

The network jet was luxurious, and it only took twenty minutes to get to the island. They'd barely taken off before they were landing. She could see the entire island from the air. A thatched-roofed cottage was nestled amongst the trees and sand. It looked like part of it jutted out over the water like a pier. Fountains bordered a sleek in-ground pool. She couldn't wait to explore her vacation home.

Mike helped her from the plane and into a waiting jeep. The house was less than a mile away. When they arrived, he'd jumped out of the jeep and grabbed her bags like they were empty before she even unbuckled her seatbelt. She'd been only one pound under the weight limit when she checked in at the airport, so she knew they weren't light. In his short-sleeved shirt his muscles looked like finely sculpted mountains.

He opened the unlocked front door then gestured for her to go inside ahead of him.

A hunk and a gentleman. If he's got brains—and he must; they don't hand out licenses to dummies—it'd be a trifecta! Pay attention, Carolyn. He just said something about keys.

"I'm sorry, I missed that," she said. "Guess I got caught up in the splendor of this place."

"It's pretty spectacular," he agreed. "I just said the keys are supposed to be in the top drawer of this chest by the door." He deposited her bags in the foyer, opened the drawer and removed a rabbit's foot with two rusty keys attached. "Yep, here they are. Looks like they haven't been used in a while." He placed them on top of the chest. There aren't any phones, but there's a radio system. I'll show you how to use it in case of an emergency."

She smiled at him. She couldn't imagine an emergency in this paradise.

After her lesson, he walked through the house with her and made sure her food and other provisions had been delivered before he prepared to leave. "Is there anything you need before I go?"

For you to go skinny-dipping with me. Whoa...where the hell had that come from?

She shook her head. She was afraid to look at him, afraid he'd see the longing in her eyes. She'd not been attracted to a man like this since she met Steve.

Always and for Never

What was wrong with her?

"If you need anything, use the radio," he reminded her. "It was nice meeting you."

After watching him drive away, she rolled her luggage to the enormous master bedroom. She quickly unpacked and put on one of her daughter's bikini's which she'd thrown in on a whim. She hadn't worn a bikini since before her children were born. She looked in the mirror. Not too shabby...well, for my age. Were bikinis this skimpy when I wore them before? More likely I didn't fill them out like this.

She grabbed a towel and headed for the pool area. It was even more spectacular picturesque at ground level than from the air. The saltwater infinity pool had a full ocean view. Carolyn dropped her towel, dove into the deep end and swam its length before emerging. She climbed the steps onto a patio facing the Pacific.

Clouds had begun to roll in more fast and furious than the waves. She'd seen some surfboards during her quick tour of the house, not that she'd dare try surfing without someone else around, or with, for that matter.

She turned a chaise to face the surf and tugged at her tiny swimsuit. She laughed. Why am I wearing this? I'm on an island—by myself. She'd unhooked and slipped off the top when she heard the doorbell ring. What? Wrapped in a towel, she moved into the shadows as she crept toward the door. She hadn't locked it. If someone was there, they could come in.

"Carolyn," she heard from inside the house, "It's Mike. I don't want to scare you."

"I'm out here," she said, walking toward him from the pool. "What's wrong?"

"I've got a problem with the plane," he said. "I need a part. I radioed and they're going to have someone bring it, but it won't be until tomorrow. There's weather coming in. Is it okay if I bunk on your couch tonight?"

Her mind was racing a mile a minute. "Does Steve know you're here?"

"I doubt it. He's at the set. The only time I interact with him is when he needs to go somewhere."

Carolyn realized he was still standing in the door. "Where are my manners? Come in, of course."

"Looks like I'm in time for sunset." He motioned to the balcony that faced west. Running the length of the house, it had access from the kitchen, living room, and bedroom. The dark clouds had parted and a kaleidoscope

Always and for Never

of colors painted the horizon. "Why don't I fix us a drink and we can watch it?"

"I'll run put on some clothes, I mean change out of this swimsuit."

"Better hurry. The sun sets fast around here."

She almost sprinted to the bedroom and locked the door. What the hell? Tossing her swimsuit and towel into the bathtub, she changed into a simple pale blue sundress. She combed out her long, wet hair, twisted it into a chignon and secured it with a clip. She put on some clear lip-gloss and reached for her mascara. What am I doing?

"Hurry," she heard him yell.

"I'm coming," she said, and then wondered if it was a prophecy.

He handed her a glass of wine, and she sank into a cushioned rattan chaise to watch an explosion of hues drop below the horizon.

"Beautiful," he said.

"Breathtaking," she agreed, but when she looked at him, he wasn't looking at the sky. He was looking at her —with those ocean blue eyes. His sun-bleached hair was a tad longer than was probably regulation for most pilots. He wasn't as tall as Steve, but he was rock solid. She would guess he was in his late forty's, maybe fifty.

She downed her wine and handed him the glass. "More, please."

He chuckled. "Liked that, huh?"

"Needed it, is more like it."

He took her glass and disappeared into the kitchen. She leaned back into her chair. Careful, girl. You've been so holier than thou about your faithfulness when Steve was out of town. Don't you dare blow it here in his own backyard with one of his employees and then rub his nose in it. Look, but don't touch.

He placed her second glass of wine and the bottle on a small, round table next to her chair before he went back to the kitchen and returned with a tray of cheese, crackers and fruit. She picked up a piece of mango and bit into it. The explosion of flavor caught her off guard. "Wow."

"Good, huh? There's fresh mahi-mahi I can throw on the grill. We could make a salad, maybe stir-fry some vegetables. I saw some locally grown yams. You want your first meal here to be memorable."

She didn't trust herself to speak, so she just nodded.

Always and for Never

He lit the tiki torches around the edges of the balcony when he put the fish on the grill. They worked together in the kitchen and fell into an easy banter. The meal was ready in what seemed like minutes.

"There must be a sound system around here somewhere," Mike said. "Ah, here it is. What do you like? Jazz? Oldies? Big Band?"

Oh my god is he trying to give me a heart attack?

"How about Michael Buble'?"

"Sounds good," she managed to croak. While Mike was fooling with the music, she'd taken the food to the table on the balcony. It was pitch dark except for the stars which exploded in the night sky. The storm had obviously gone elsewhere. She could hear the surf and see the white caps of the waves between the dancing branches of the palm trees.

He'd opened another bottle of wine when he joined her. He poured them each a glass and offered a toast. "May you have the vacation of your dreams and may your memories last a lifetime."

Is he making a pass at me? Hell, it's been so long, I don't even know how to recognize the signs. I do know I'd better go easy on the wine, though this is delicious.

Inkception Books

During dinner, he kept her amused with his stories. He'd been a Navy pilot, but his first wife hadn't liked military life. He didn't blame her. He hadn't particularly liked it either, but he got to fly cool planes. After his twenty years, he retired. He remarried and flew commercial jets. He'd thought he had a good marriage—until he came home and found his wife in bed with their neighbor...another woman.

Carolyn could tell this betrayal had hurt him deeply, but the way he told the story had her wiping tears of laughter from her cheeks. He said he'd sworn off matrimony, retired long before he hit the airline's mandatory retirement age and now saw the world on the network's dime.

When he asked about her marriage and family, she kept her answers general and positive. She didn't know this man, and he worked for Steve. Certain protocols had to be observed. She did, however, tell him about her foray back into the professional arena and shared a couple of funny stories of her own. He asked about her business model, the progress she'd made and where she hoped to be in a year. She'd completed a few small jobs since Steve had left and had signed a contract to do a

Always and for Never

whole house that was under construction. He asked good questions. More importantly, he listened – really listened to her answers and gave her positive feedback and affirmations.

"Wait here," he said, abruptly.

"I'm not going anywhere. Except maybe to sleep." She'd moved from the table back to a chaise . "The sound of those waves and this ocean breeze might lull me into dreamland."

"Go ahead. I'll wake you if you start drooling."

She laughed. He felt like an old friend.

"On second thought, I won't," he added, as he walked into the house. "I'll just take the bed."

The mention of the bed was like someone had thrown a bucket of cold water in her face. He's not asking me to go to bed with him; he said he'd take the bed. Get a grip. Steve's going to be pissed, but I've done nothing wrong. Though I wouldn't mind...Carolyn! Stop!

Mike returned to the patio carrying two brownies topped with vanilla ice cream and cherries. She threw her head back and laughed. Here she thought he was trying to seduce her, and he was making dessert.

The heavy sweets almost did her in. After a long

day of travel, she could barely keep her eyes open.

"You look like you're losing the battle," Mike said. "Why don't you turn in? I'll clean up."

"You're sure?" she asked, praying he was.

"I don't have jet lag. I'll take it from here. Sweet dreams."

She retreated to the beautifully appointed master bedroom and locked the door. Then she unlocked it, then locked it again. There was a half bath off the foyer, so she didn't have to worry about him needing to use her bathroom during the night. She took a long shower and crawled between the crisp, white sheets. She thought she'd be asleep before her head hit the pillow, but she tossed and turned, trying to get comfortable. She could hear Mike singing along with Harry Connick, Jr. Suddenly there was a loud crash followed by a string of expletives.

She grabbed her robe and rushed through the living room to the kitchen where he stood, surrounded by broken dishes, cutlery, food—a real mess. And, his hand was dripping blood on top of it all.

"What happened?"

"I cut my freaking hand."

Always and for Never

"I can see that. You need to rinse it off and put pressure on it."

"I can't move, unless you want to see more blood. There's glass everywhere, and I'm barefoot."

"Where are your shoes?"

"By the front door."

She ran back to her bedroom for her own shoes then retrieved his. After helping him slip them onto his feet, she maneuvered him to the sink and pushed his hand under a stream of running water. The slash was long but not deep.

"You'll live." She found some gauze in the hall closet and skillfully wrapped his hand. "What happened?"

Mike blushed. "I took a tray out so I could bring everything inside in one trip."

"And how'd that work out for you?" She teased.

"I was...um...kind of singing and dancing, I guess, and I thought I'd try holding it over my head with one hand like servers in restaurants do...it doesn't look that hard...well, I got off balance, and it started falling, and I grabbed something...I'm not even sure what ...and cut my hand. Then I was stuck in the middle of all this." It looked like everything they'd had on the patio was now on the kitchen floor.

"Are you drunk?"

"No." He answered a little too quickly. "I finished the bottle of wine we'd started, but that's all. We've had plenty to eat. I'm not even tipsy."

She started laughing. "I wish I had a video of this. I bet it'd win America's Funniest Home Videos."

"We aren't in America," he said, which made her laugh harder. Soon both had tears running down their faces.

"Do you have any other clothes?" she asked. "Because you're a mess."

"Yeah, I have my bag in the jeep. I didn't want to freak you out by bringing it in."

"Go get it." She waved him off. "I'll clean up the kitchen, while you take a shower and get cleaned up." She was still laughing when he walked out the front door. At least that makes him less sexy. It's more like something my son or one of his friends would do—just what I needed for perspective.

Carolyn found herself humming along with the stereo, as she turned the dishwasher on, not that there were many dishes left to wash. She'd already mopped the

Always and for Never

floor—twice. She opened another bottle of wine and poured herself a glass before she headed back to the patio chaise. The combination of the surf, the breeze, and the stars—damn, it was romantic. This would be good for her and Steve. Their marriage needed a place like this.

She heard Mike before she saw him. When she saw him, he took her breath away. Dressed only in pajama bottoms, he had a glass of wine in one hand. His abdomen was as solid as a professional football player's. He sat next to her and neither said a word through several songs.

He stood, reached for her hand and said, "Dance with me."

When she seemed to hesitate, he said, "Please...just dance with me."

She took his hand. His gaze never left hers as he pulled her into his arms. They danced through three CDs without uttering a sound. This was not her imagination. This was definitely mutual.

Finally, she leaned her head back and said, "I can't."

"I know." He cradled her head against his chest. "And I am so sorry."

"I'm sorry too...because I wish I could."

"Carolyn," he whispered into her ear, "you are special...very special. And I hate this. I hope one day you'll forgive me."

She pulled away from him, but he pulled her back so she was forced to talk into his ear. Does he not want to look me in the eyes? "Forgive you for what? What are you talking about? You sound a little crazy."

"Trust me," he whispered. "I'm not crazy...just trust me. Soon you'll understand. I promise. When this dance is over, I want you to go to bed...alone."

Carolyn felt like she'd been sucker punched. This had been the most romantic evening of her life, and she hadn't even been kissed. Had she planned to cheat on her husband? Absolutely not. Would she, under these circumstances? You bet. Now, he was dismissing her. If she weren't so tired she could fall asleep on her feet, she'd really be pissed. As it was, she'd have to think about it later.

When the song ended, Carolyn yawned. "I'm calling it a night. Goodnight." Without even looking back, she went to the bedroom and locked the door. When she crawled between the sheets that time, she went to sleep immediately.

Always and for Never

~

Carolyn was alone when she awoke the next morning. She walked on the beach, sat by the pool and tried to figure out what the hell had happened the night before. She finally decided Mike had realized he worked for her husband and sleeping with her could cost him his job if they got caught. Or maybe he was being gallant and didn't want to jeopardize her thirty-year marriage. Those were the only logical explanations. It didn't explain his odd conversation, but that was the best she could do.

She was surprised when her husband showed up later that day. She thought it'd be at least a couple more. Steve told her to get dolled up—they had the wrap party to fly back for. He said they'd finished all of the segments. The network had loved them and planned to run the show during prime time in the fall.

She wore a flowered sundress and grabbed a lightweight shawl. Red strappy high-heeled sandals with a matching handbag completed her outfit. For jewelry, she kept it simple and classy with pearls. Because time was limited, she pulled her auburn hair atop her head, twisted it into a loose bun and pulled out tresses to give it a more casual look.

"My God," Steve said. "You look beautiful. You actually glow."

"Must be the sun, or it could be you haven't seen me in months."

"I've been on this island with gorgeous women," he said. "None could hold a candle to you tonight."

The compliment warmed her, and she cozied up against him. "Can't we skip the dinner and go ahead and start our vacation?"

He chuckled. "I wish. Tomorrow. I promise. Tonight I show you off. Pack a bag. We'll spend the night there, then come back here first thing tomorrow. It'll be a late night. This promises to be some shindig."

With her overnight bag, Carolyn joined him at the jeep where a stunning Polynesian woman stood waiting.

"Honey, this is Alana, our pilot."

After pleasantries, they took off with Carolyn and Steve settled in the comfort of the back.

"Do you require all of your pilots to be drop-dead gorgeous?"

Always and for Never

Steve laughed. "She is pretty, isn't she? And, now that you mention it, I guess Mike's a nice-looking guy."

"Nice-looking? Steve, he's what they used to call movie star handsome."

"Oh, do I need to be jealous?"

She felt herself flush. "Of course not, but there is something you do need to know."

"I'm listening."

"He had trouble with his plane after he dropped me off. A storm was brewing. He couldn't get a part flown in until this morning, so he spent last night on my couch."

Steve coughed.

"Now, before you go down your usual path about me being alone with a man, especially one you know I find attractive, let me assure you I slept in the bed, and he slept on the sofa. We did eat dinner together. It would've been silly not to."

Steve smiled. He almost looked smug. "Oh, I believe you. And, furthermore, I've decided I trust you in your clients' homes, too. It's business after all."

"I'm happy to hear this, but did you get hit in the head with a coconut? We've argued about this for months and just as suddenly as you decided I couldn't be trusted

Inkception Books

you decide I can? Did you have another dream?"

He laughed. "No dreams."

"This isn't getting you out of therapy, you know. That was our deal."

"I agreed to it," he said. "I'll go...for at least a month."

"Steve, have you been having an affair? Is that what this bizarre behavior has been all about?"

"Of course not. I'm offended you'd even ask."

"You've been asking me for months. I'm just trying to make sense out of a crazy time in our marriage."

"You'll get clarity, soon, my love. I have, and you will too."

As soon as the plane landed, they were whisked away to the event where they hobnobbed at a cocktail party before a seated dinner. The chairman of the network was the M.C. He thanked everyone who worked on the new series and received a hearty round of applause. When he announced the network planned to air the series on Tuesdays at nine, he got a standing ovation.

Carolyn was clueless. She still knew almost nothing about the show. It was a reality series...that was about it. She didn't even know its name.

Always and for Never

Steve took her hand under the table, leaned over and said, "I love you." More odd behavior.

When the lights dimmed and the show's premise and clips were revealed, it all crystallized for her. The reality show was to see if partners were faithful. One partner was set-up—placed in a romantic setting with an attractive actor, she guessed, and their every movement, their every word, was taped. It was carefully edited, but it was taped.

And, she'd been one of the victims...one of the few, shown at the screening, who had passed the test. The episodes were cleverly done. The actors knew their marks, knew the vulnerabilities of their prey, and played them like violins.

The lights came up to thunderous applause. Steve looked like the cat that had eaten the canary. "I'm so proud of you. And, if you wouldn't cheat on me in that situation, I can let go of my whole phobia of you cheating on me, period. I see how silly it was anyway."

Carolyn gritted her teeth. She was afraid to say anything because of the anger that festered inside of her. She was afraid to get up and walk from the room because she wasn't sure her legs would support her. So, she sat, staring at her husband, a man she thought she knew, a man who had surely lost his mind.

When most of the people were gone, she ventured to their limousine and went to their hotel. She phoned the airlines and changed her reservations to the next flight home. All of her clothes were on the island, but he could send them. She had her passport with her. That was all she had to have. She had to get out of there.

The door opened, and Steve walked in. "Baby, I was worried. Why didn't you tell me you were leaving?"

"I'm leaving," she said.

"No, I mean at the dinner."

"I mean you," she said. "I'm leaving you. I don't care if we have been married almost thirty years, what you did to me is unforgivable."

"But, I did it because I love you. Don't you see? I had to prove to myself you were being faithful."

"And you couldn't just trust me? After thirty years, you couldn't trust me? Instead, you set me up, filmed and exploited me for one of your reality television shows, which, by the way, is not going to happen. If you try to air an advertisement or episode with me in it, I'll sue you; I'll sue the network, I'll make you wish you'd nev-

Always and for Never

er even met me."

"But, baby, I love you! Isn't there anything I can do?"

"Yeah," she said. "You can move out of my way. You're blocking the door."

fractured love story

by Lisa Berryhill

Looking out over the sea of bright shiny new cowboy hats around the bar, Laura doubted any of these wannabes had ever even ridden a horse. That damn John Travolta movie had attracted way too many posers to Houston. Why would anybody with a brain want to be a roughneck who lived in a trailer with Debra Winger? She was supposed to be a raging bitch if you believed the tabloids.

But then who did? Thinking about tabloids made her look over at Bobby, an old hell-raising buddy she hadn't seen much since high school. Bobby had always been a dedicated reader of those rags and a good

Always and for Never

source of the latest alien conspiracy. At the moment he seemed laser-focused on the action behind the bar. "So what do you think about Debra Winger? Is she really hard to work with?"

"Huh? How would I know?" he mumbled, still watching the bartender who was working the opposite end of the bar. In Laura's opinion, this was definitely a change for the better. They'd finally hired a good-looking bartender, one hotter than the sand on Galveston Beach in July. All those muscles and shoulder length sun bleached hair. Must be a body builder who loved the outdoors.

"I could handle the outdoors if I also got to handle that..." Laura said out loud without thinking.

Bobby glanced sideways at Laura. She knew he could tell she was salivating over the hot stuff behind the bar. They'd been inseparable in high school but lost touch during their college days. A lot changed when you got away from your hometown. Hell, even her hometown had morphed into something she barely recognized. It was still a humid, paved over bayou that smelled like the ship channel but the people seemed different. Instead of hearing the familiar twangy Texas drawl you heard accents from all over the country—heck, from all over the world—as you walked down the street. Even La Carafe, Laura and Bobby's favorite bar, was showing signs of an invasion of the drugstore cowboys.

Located in one of the only remaining original buildings downtown, La Carafe had a traditional shotgun saloon layout. The bar took up most of the narrow main level with room for only a few two-top tables along the side of the room with a round five-seat table near the restroom where the classic jukebox sat. Outside in the back corner there was a small, enclosed courtyard reminiscent of New Orleans. Upstairs was a private party room that in the modern age was a mirror image of the bottom floor. Back in the wild-west days it was lined with narrow cots for the working girls to use when they enticed actual cowboys to spend some of their hard-earned cattle driving money for rides of a different sort. Plenty of history…or likely herstory…had been made here.

"Hey, where you think the new guy is from? Definitely not a Texan, I'd say." Bobby looked at her expectantly.

Laura tore her eyes from the barkeep's well-done buns to ask, "Why do you say that?"

Always and for Never

"Haven't you heard him chatting up the patrons? That's some kind of Yankee accent. Boston, maybe. Or New York."

Laura, deciding this was her chance to get the attention of the gorgeous Fabio look-alike, called across the bar. "Hey, surfer dude, settle a bet for us, would ya?" He actually glided over to them. Laura wondered how a body that sculpted could move so smoothly. "My friend here said you must be from Boston with that accent. I'm betting on New York, specifically Brooklyn. Who's right?"

Bobby threw Laura a quizzical glance that turned into a look of understanding. "Yeah," he said. "Boston, right?"

"Nah, both youse guys are wrong, but the pretty lady is closest. I'm from Long Island." He said it as if it was one long word. "Name's Daniel Barrone, but most people call me Danny." He extended a meaty hand first to Laura and then to Bobby as they offered their names. "What about you two? Where're you from?"

Laura said, "Right here." Bobby stumbled through his answer, mentioning his college days at Clemson while still claiming Houston as his hometown.

"Hah! So are you guys rare native Houstonians?"

Now that he was closer, Laura could see that Danny's eyes were hazel like her own. And he was short like her. They were both blonde, too. It crossed her mind maybe this attraction was a bit narcissistic, but she quickly decided she didn't give a damn if it was. This guy was just too yummy.

Bobby, weirdly tongue-tied, sputtered some single syllables bordering on grunts. Then he let out what could only be described as a giggle. Laura shot him a questioning look that clearly said "WTF?" He excused himself as he headed toward the jukebox.

Danny turned back to Laura. "So what's with your boyfriend? Seems kinda nervous." Laura frowned and said, "Oh no no no no no! Bobby is a friend, not my boyfriend." She surprised herself when a cross between a giggle and a hiccup escaped her lips, and her hand flew up to her mouth. She glimpsed her face in the mirror behind the bar and saw that it was redder than a chili pepper. She only hoped Danny found it attractive. The jukebox started playing Edith Piaf's "La Vie En Rose" just as the other bartender called Danny to the opposite side of the bar.

Always and for Never

~

The next time Laura saw Danny she was on a date with a French chef she had met during Sunday brunch at a friend's home in the artsy Montrose section of town. The guy seemed fine in the light of day in a crowd, but Laura found him a bit angry and intense one on one. Can you say Incredible Hulk? "Damn, of all the times for Kathie to bail on me," she thought. It was Laura's practice never to get into a guy's car on the first date. Experience had taught her that it was better to maintain a little distance and a lot of control until she was sure about the man. She had arrived at this plan after what could best be called several close calls.

Tonight her friend Kathie, a transplant from Nebraska, had asked—no, begged—to come along. She also insisted on driving. Then she developed a "headache" and went home early. That left Laura at the literal mercy of Frankie or Francoise or whatever the hell name this Nouvelle Cuisine Julia Child knock-off went by. was called.

Laura knew she was in trouble when he led her to his black, jacked-up Chevy Camaro with dual exhausts. It had four on the floor and blackened windows. Plus when she sat down, the first thing she saw was a spiked dog collar hanging off the rear view mirror. Handcuffs dangled from the gearshift.

As Francoise put on his leather driving gloves (pretentious, anyone?), he started telling her she just had to try the thirty-year-old single malt scotch he had at his house. But this wasn't Laura's first rodeo. She countered by being ever so charming as she gently walked her fingers up his chest and over his face. Then she purred in her thickest Southern accent, "Oh now, darlin', you must let me take you to Houston's oldest and most quaint bar, La Carafe. It was once a famous bordello, and it still has the ambiance of those old times. It's an incredible rush!"

As they headed downtown, she breathed a quiet sigh of relief. La Carafe had always been her safe place and, by going there, she was hoping she could figure out a way to slip out of the Hulk's grasp without him busting out of those already too tight leather pants.

It was getting close to last call when they arrived. The place was deserted except for a drunken ship captain sitting at the bar. To Laura's delight, Danny was polishing wine glasses. "Hey, Danny! How's it going tonight? Good

Always and for Never

to see you, as always." She figured if Frankie thought she and the hunky bartender were tight things might go more smoothly when she ditched him.

Laura ordered her usual Chardonnay while her companion asked for a wine list. Danny chuckled and said, "We nevah saw the need fa one. We got wine and beeah—domestic beeah, by the way. Just name ya poison."

"Poison is right," Francoise said in his heaviest French accent. "Come, Mademoiselle Laura, we are leaving this gauche establishment."

The look on Laura's face must have telegraphed her feelings. "Ummm, I don't think so," she said. "I just got my wine, and I want to finish it. But you go on; I can call a cab."

Later Laura would reflect that her encounter with the Hulk began in slow motion. Chef Francoise tried to grab her wrist when she stepped toward the jukebox. As she twirled away, he tossed the five-top table to the side, flipping it over as he tried to grab her around the waist.

"I bought you a delicious dinner, and now you will come home with me!" He actually roared. Francoise continued moving toward Laura, backing her into the corner next to the jukebox. He squeezed past the upturned table, reaching for her wrist again, this time with his left hand.

That's when time went into hyper speed for Laura. She watched a look of pain and sheer terror cross the chef's face as Danny twisted his right arm pinning it behind him. His eyes bulged as he struggled to loosen Danny's hold.

The Hulk himself couldn't have turned any greener.

"Da lady told you she ain't goin' with ya. I think it's best if ya take ya skinny French ass on home alone, Pepe Le Pew."

Danny picked him up by his belt, half marching and half carrying him toward La Carafe's door.

~

After the dust settled and the door was locked, Laura took off her heels and put her feet up on the bar stool next to her. "Whew, that was intense. I appreciate you coming to my rescue, Danny. I don't like coming

Always and for Never

across like some damsel in distress, but when I do find myself in times of trouble, I sure wish you could always be my Prince Charming."

"Ya... gotta be more careful, Laura. Guys aren't all bad, but the assholes leave behind a wide trail of broken women."

Oh, those dreamy hazel eyes of his. Laura melted into the bar stool. She tried hard not to swoon. "You have to let me take you to dinner to thank you for saving me from the Marquis de Sade. I insist! But no French restaurants."

That was the way it began, with Laura asking Danny out.

Before long they went everywhere together. Occasionally, when Danny suggested it, they would include Bobby, and it seemed like old times to Laura. So what if Danny was the shy type who didn't even try to kiss her? She really enjoyed the hugs and holding hands. There was something to be said for taking it slow.

Anticipation could be delicious.

~

Inkception Books

Laura could barely contain her excitement. Danny's dear friend, Earl, was celebrating a special birthday (one ending in a zero) and Danny wanted to throw a party for all his friends. Not only did Laura get to play hostess—a role all Southern women are born for—she would also get introduced to Danny's closest friends. So what if they were mostly men he worked out with? She always enjoyed being the only woman in a group of guys. Danny had insisted on including Bobby, so that meant Laura would have at least one familiar face at the party.

As she drove up to Danny's duplex apartment, she saw him outside wrestling with a large piece of cardboard. He was trying to spell out "Happy Birthday, Earl!" using multi-colored Christmas lights. It wasn't working, but he'd never looked sexier bending over the "artwork." Laura felt a strong urge to grab him, throw him to the ground and have her way with him. She couldn't help but notice Danny's neighbor from across the street also taking in the view. She felt a wave of jealousy. "Woah," she thought, "What's wrong with me? It's not like we're in a committed relationship or anything. On top of that, it's hypocritical." Laura's personal philosophy had always been 'If I'm still breathing, I'm looking.'

Always and for Never

She settled for one of Danny's crushing bear hugs, trying her best to melt into his body in a way that had made the men in her past putty in her, uh, hands. But it seemed as if Danny was immune to her physical charms and desires. Maybe he was just focused on the damn lights. That had to be it.

Perhaps if she helped Danny hurry and finish the sign they might have time for their own little private pre-party celebration inside. "Here, let me lend a hand with that. I think I can sketch the words out and then we can punch holes from the back to put the lights through. We might even be able to use the flasher bulb and make the lights twinkle."

When they'd completed the sign, Danny was quite impressed with her craftiness. "Wow! That looks fabulous! Almost like a professional did it."

"Stick with me, Handsome, and I'll gladly show you how professional I am." Laura could not believe she had said that. And in a husky voice no less. God, she must really be horny to resort to that. Still, after a month of hugs, handholding, and kisses on the cheek how could she not be in full-tilt lust?

As they climbed the stairs, Danny was running

down the names of people he had invited to the party so they could get a head count. After listening to a long list populated by male names, Laura asked, "So will I be the only woman at tonight's festivities? I wouldn't complain a bit, mind you—just wondering what type of people I'll be meeting."

Danny turned around to face her. He gave her that twisted grin she had come to know so well. "This is a really special party, Laura. It's what ya might call a fruit and nuts party."

"Fruit and nuts party? Are you kidding me? I made a bunch of finger foods, but none with fruits or nuts. What do you mean?"

Danny stopped on the landing. "What I mean is you'll either be a fruit or a nut if you come."

Laura's grin was more confused than amused.

~

Laura had bought a new, sexy outfit for the party—a sheer black blouse with a hot pink bustier underneath that showed off two of her best assets. A pair of red satin pants trimmed with black mink cuffs and stilettos com-

Always and for Never

pleted the not-so-subtle ensemble. She was feeling pretty foxy as she stepped into the hallway.

Danny did a double take when he saw her. "Girl, ya look like you're ready to go clubbin' at Numbers or even Metropolitan in that getup."

"Oh, I'm ready for something." Laura squeezed past Danny rubbing up against him like a kitty cat. "Hope you are, too, Danny Darlin'." She was counting on her long, slow wink to seal the deal.

The first guest to arrive was Bobby. He looked quite dashing in a three-piece white suit with a black shirt. Shades of John Travolta again. Laura just couldn't escape that guy. After giving Laura a hug, Bobby waved at Danny. Odd. He seemed a little shy. Before she knew it, Danny bounded across the room and gave Bobby the same kind of bear hug she'd thought was reserved for her. "Oh well," she said under her breath. "I should just be glad my fellows are friends!"

The doorbell rang again, and Laura answered it. Standing there was a long tall drink of water that could easily pass for Freddy Mercury but with better teeth. "Well, hello there. I'm Laura, Danny's....friend." Laura smiled and stepped back, motioning the handsome guy inside.

He sashayed into the room. That's the only way you could describe his entrance. He was wearing a cape draped dramatically around his shoulders. In his right hand, held high above his head, was a cake with purple frosting and pink flowers.

As he swept further into the apartment, Danny came out of the kitchen. The new party guest set the cake on the table with the other food and proceeded to grab Danny by the head as he planted what was obviously a very affectionate French kiss on his mouth.

Laura fell onto the sofa trying to keep her head from spinning. She began to review the many hours she had spent with Danny. The trips to the Flea Market where they both favored 70's kitsch, the musicals at the Alley Theater, the clubs where they always managed to dance in groups. Never once did they go to a romantic dinner or make out in the car. And all this time she had convinced herself that Danny was just shy. Anticipation my ass.

While Bobby was being introduced to Mr. Dramatic, Laura slipped past them into the bathroom. She grabbed the sides of the old-fashioned sink and stared

Always and for Never

into the mirror.

Looking straight into her wide, startled eyes, she asked herself one question: "Okay, Miss Sophistication, now what?"

She reviewed her options. She could cry but, damn, her makeup looked so good. She could hide in the bathtub or just slip out and go home but what a waste of her great sexy outfit.

Wait, what? A waste. Wasn't that what this last month had been? All the time she had thought things were heating up between her and Danny when in reality she was not and never would be what he wanted. Oh, God, what a fool she had been.

There was a knock at the bathroom door. "Just a minute," she croaked.

"Laura, it's me, Bobby. Can I come in?"

"I guess so. You've seen me angry, drunk and disappointed before. Two out of three ain't bad, according to Meatloaf."

"Ah, Laura, I've wanted to tell you so many times. I just couldn't find the words."

"Bobby! It wasn't your place to tell me that Danny is gay. That was for him to share."

"Laura, you don't understand. I wasn't trying to tell you that Danny is gay. I wanted to tell you that I am."

She looked at her old friend as if seeing him clearly for the first time and saw someone she had always loved and cherished. She felt ashamed that she had not been there for him to confide in.

"Ah, dear Bobby, all that matters to me is that you be the happiest Bobby you can be. Whatever that means to you, that's what's important. And you know what? That's exactly what I'm going out there to tell Danny."

"Are you sure you want to stay at the party, Laura? I can take you home and we could just hang out if you want. I happen to have my "Urban Cowboy" DVD with me," he said with a twinkle in his eye.

"Not on your life, Bobby. Danny told me that if you were a guest at this party, you were either a fruit or a nut. Well, I'm going out there and show them all that I'm a little of both. So come on, John Travolta. We're not looking for love in all the wrong places anymore. Tonight we're staying alive!"

penelope's handbag

by Jennifer Steen

Restaurant. There were fish in a tank right over the booth. The decorations inside the tank looked too bright like either circus midgets had purchased them or children made them. The brightness seemed to beam down like a spotlight onto the table and the Asian food. Penelope wasn't quite sure what form of Asian the food would be. She wasn't sophisticated enough to know the difference between the different kinds, but she had an inkling that this was an expensive place.

The handbag, which she had purchased at a garage sale, had a stain on one side, and 'Rachael' etched on it in giant gold letters. It would not fit very well in this setting. And it wasn't her name. She had begun to feel self-conscious about it as soon as she had walked in and been seated by a suit-coated waiter. The feeling of shame intensified as they took her drink order, and as her blind date arrived and stared down at the twenty-page menu. He gripped it tightly as though it were an enthralling novel.

Why doesn't he look at me? Maybe it's the purse.

As stealthily as possible she took her foot and shoved the bag further under the table.

His name was Bryan, and he had sandy blonde hair which was combed back. He would have been an incredible catch, good for a month at least, but then he crossed his legs, and one boot stuck out from the table cloth. A cowboy boot.

What does he think I am? A rodeo? Cowboy boots? Why those? What was he saying with that choice? He couldn't be a serious catch now; cowboys tended to be dirty, smokers, and homophobic. Despite her disappointment, she tried to make pleasant conversation while they wrestled down the foreign appetizer.

She began awkwardly, "I love that they have bright tanks over the tables."

Always and for Never

He ignored her altogether staring at a passing waitress for five seconds. A silent storm of thinking was let loose in Penelope's mind.

Why isn't he looking at me? Why? Am I not pretty? Am I not interesting and fun? Are my boobs too small? Does he prefer redheads or brunettes? Am I not valuable, like he doesn't respect me because there is a stain on my purse? No, of course not, he doesn't know about that, only I do. Well, perhaps he can tell...I'm slumping like an insecure girl like that one girl did in high school. She would slump her shoulders and people would call her names. I swear to God I am just going to get in my car and drive away and never come back.

Then finally he came out of his distracted thinking. "So, let's say that a man was once found to have a Barbie cup on his desk, do you think other people would see him as a gay person?"

Confusion took over her demeanor. She felt like she was trying to interpret this question as though he had asked it in a foreign language.

That was a story question. Confusing. "I'm sorry?"

"Do you think a man like that would be seen as a

gay person?"

"Well..." Was this a trick question? Like to see if she was homophobic?

She didn't care about the true answer, just about the answer he wanted her to give. He looked at her hoping for something; perhaps it was assurance. Was he this person, the man with the cup? Was he on this date to assure himself of his own sexuality? Or, perhaps he was an ultraconservative cowboy trying to trap her into admitting any liberal leanings.

She needed more time. "Could you repeat the question?"

Let's see... he's rich, he wears cowboy boots, he is probably a homophobe.

"Do you think a man who allowed a Barbie cup to touch his desk one time is homosexual?"

"Um...yes."

"Oh..." He looked back into his menu seeming very sad.

"But I mean," she corrected, "that can be kind of sexy."

"Barbie cups or being homosexual?"

"Both?"

Always and for Never

He laughed. And then he laughed more. More again. Way too much. He slapped the table with his hand and then pounded with a fist. This was completely uncomfortable. She grabbed up her purse to dig through it and pretend to look for something. Then she remembered the stain and the name on it and dropped it back under her feet again.

His laughter stopped. Now there was nothing to talk about. They stared at the table. Was all of this social torture worth a free meal? The awkward pauses, the questions, the circus midget colored fish?

She had to find something to say, anything to break this awkward pause. "Those are really bright colors in the tank. Right over your hair. I think they are in fashion. This is a very fashionable place to eat at, I think."

For some reason, that statement felt extremely awkward. She felt dumb.

Penelope stared at her skirt which was tweed from the seventies and felt a great desire to take that man list out of her purse and cross Bryan's name right off. Who cared about fashionable fish tanks? He was a total jerk. Online dating may have provided Penelope with an assortment of options, but options were one thing--quali-

Inkception Books

ty something else.

"So Penelope," and he emphasized her name as if it were a code word for something, "do you have more than one Loveland account?"

She paused considering the implications of such a question. "No."

"Do you perhaps dye your hair on a regular basis? Move from town to town? Do you bring your camera into movie theaters and casinos?"

"No."

"Penelope. What kind of name is that?"

"What is it with you and all of these questions?"

"I thought you were kind of cute on Monday, but now it's Friday, and I'm not entirely sure you aren't a made-up person."

"I'm not a liar. I don't lie."

"If you don't, then why did you feel the need to state that twice?"

She tried to change the subject. "These menus are like novels..."

"Penelope, if that is your real name, why did you really meet me here tonight? Was it to seduce me with your feminine wiles and then take my car stereo or drill

118

Always and for Never

me for information about Bank and Loan, while I hang from that new lighted bridge over the river?"

"Why are you accusing me of weird stuff?"

"Why? I'll tell you why!"

Bryan kicked the purse out from under the table. It slid across the tile with a horrendous jingle. "Because you are carrying a purse that says Rachael!"

Humiliation soaked through her skin, coloring it a brilliant scarlet. She kicked it back under the table glancing around at the other people. Then in a hushed fury, she leaned forward to answer his ridiculous question, "It cost me a penny at a garage sale."

"You expect me to believe that a beautiful, accomplished, thin, doe-eyed blonde like you is going to purposely carry a named purse into a sophisticated restaurant with a name on it that isn't her own?"

"Leave my purse out of this! Okay, fine. Maybe I do have a few Loveland accounts. But my name is Penelope."

"Why have you been lying to me for five days?"

"I didn't say anything when I saw your cowboy boots. I think we're even."

"What else is wrong with you? I'm not saying we

won't have a relationship which might involve sex--because I am a totally heterosexual man who is not afraid of women--but I think if there are any other skeletons in this closet, that I should know about them."

"I don't have any skeletons. Except for the three people I killed." She laughs maniacally hoping he will get the joke. He doesn't.

"And..."

"And... I sleep in a boat."

"You live on a boat?"

"No, I sleep in one."

"Why?"

"Because I didn't have room for the bed."

"Why did you need a boat?"

"Why don't I need a boat? It was free!"

"Are you a hoarder?"

"No, I'm a junker. There's a big difference."

"Junker? What's that?"

"I junk."

"Based on where you have placed this word in the sentence I am lead to believe this is a verb, however, I have never heard such a syntactic structure before."

"I junk. I buy junk. I obsess over the piles of free,

Always and for Never

used, and potentially damaged items, but which also have the capacity to bring joy to the downtrodden."

"Isn't that what hoarders do?"

"No, and I'm offended by your tone...hoarders have many things. I only want to.

"Junk is junk. What opportunity?"

"To get something new...without paying for it."

"But it's junk."

"It's free."

"Don't you have money?"

"I went to college. I don't have any money."

"I don't think there is any way that I can believe you at this point."

"Why?"

"Because you steal people's trash."

The waiter arrived with their orders. The food steamed, and they glared at each other through the swirls of moisture.

Finally, Penelope picked up her fork and began to twirl her noodles.

"Typical."

"What! What am I doing wrong? Is my fork positioned wrong? Do my eyes look too glazed over with fury?

Do I still smell like my five dogs?"

She stared him down demanding him answer with her eyes, but he leaned away from her.

"No. I suppose I'm a little surprised that you would force yourself to sit here after all of this. But of course you won't text me again, and you will delete me out of your phone."

"Possibly."

"Possibly? Oh right, you are just saying that to make me feel better."

"Well, since I'm being completely honest here, I'm just here for the food. I'm poor. And there are all kinds of men who want to take me out to dinner. And I don't have to sleep with them or anything." Then he looks down at his menu again in a sort of disappointment.

Sour After Hours

the fallen leaves

by Pragya Vishnoi

She entered the park. Dead leaves were fluttering like memories of bygone days. Just like those memories, those fallen leaves were also looking beautiful with their splendid rusty color glowing in the wounded light of the setting sun. She had come to visit her sister's grandchildren in this city. The idea of spending her seventy-first winter all by herself in her home at the hills was not very welcoming for her.

Sometimes she regretted her decision of not marrying when loneliness appeared to suffocate her. But if she had married, what was the guarantee that she was not left to spend her old days alone like her younger sister when her children left their nests to explore career oppor-

Always and for Never

tunities in the wide sky of world? And it was not her decision to not marry. It was simply a matter of chance. The men who appeared suitable to her had rejected her; and she had rejected those who considered her suitable.

It was not that she was a career woman. Yes, she was financially independent, but she didn't fit the definition of an ambitious person. This was especially strange in those times when a woman could either be a homemaker or a very successful professional. Except those two paths, no trail was considered appropriate for a girl. But she never took those paths. She never tried too hard to push her career forward as she believed- Dreams are for life, life is not for dreams. If one's dreams prevent her from experiencing even the simple joys, they are not worth pursuing. Was this philosophy correct or not- who knows?

But why was she questioning her life now? Why was she regretting when it was of no use? She consoled herself that happiness depends on only one decision- Whether you want to be happy or not? All other decisions are trivial.

She looked all around her. Children were playing. Their mothers were telling them not to go too far or else they wouldn't be able to play games on their tablets that night. She smiled. When she was child, they were told, "If you go too far, the bad man will kidnap you and take you in his den." "Children have become smart now", she thought sadly, "They won't fall in these traps now, in the times when the threat has become a reality." A girl and boy with bags on their shoulders were talking quietly, walking hand in hand. "They should have bunked their tuition classes. Some things never change. Except the fact that in these times, both will come here again after three-four months, only there partners will be different," she giggled.

    Then her eyes fell on an old man sitting on a bench in the corner. He was looking dignified in his black coat with carefully combed hair. And his eyes were sea-green, which reminded her of someone buried in the deepest layer of her memory.

    "Can it possibly be...him?" she said to herself. He was not the only person in the world with sea-green eyes but she had not seen many people having eyes of the same color as the sea sparkling under the playful sun.

    She pretended to have a walk in the park so that she could get a close look of his face. She went past him,

Always and for Never

honoring him with a fleeting glance...Her cheeks which were left colorless by age were shyly gaining their long-lost pinkish shade.

It was indeed him...her teenage crush whom she had not seen once in the last fifty-four years. His features had not changed much making it easy for her to recognize him. "He has only grown a little old," she told herself.

Now she was really glad that she had not married. Had she been married, she could not look at him like now, without any guilt. Had he taken a wife? She wanted to ask him. She suddenly started feeling the heat of envy towards a woman she did not know. A woman who may not even exist. Who knows whether she existed or not? It was possible that he too was unmarried. After all, he was always a rebel. She consoled herself. She didn't want to let that precious moment burn in jealousy.

She tried to remember why she was attracted to him. He was not very handsome. Neither was he the classic serious-looking topper-the kind of person whom she could like. He was quite the opposite- the popular, attention seeking one, that kind of person who disgusted her before she met him. But, well, love is another name of unpredictability.

She couldn't help thinking what would have happened, if she had confessed her love for him. Maybe he could have rejected her. No she was not that bad. Although she was not in the popular squad, people used to say that she was beautiful. Thinking this, she carelessly tossed her snow white tresses like she used to do with her cascading black hair in her teens.

Maybe, they could've married and, her attraction for him could have possibly been inundated in the realities of life. She had seen many times that one is attracted to a thing until he doesn't get it. The moment he gets it, that thing becomes worthless for him. The thing which seems diamond to a person becomes a useless stone after he gets it.

Only if she had a parallel life, she could check this theory by going back in time and marrying him.

Wait...he had turned. Was he looking in her direction? Had he recognized her? She looked at her curly lock of hair, which annoyingly persisted disrupting her view. Not many people back in her native hilly town had curly hair. In fact, in her whole class, she was the only one with curly hair. Then, people could not change their

Always and for Never

appearance by cosmetic treatments like now. Everyone used to have their own uniqueness. Earlier she used to complain that her hair was not like her friends. But now, she was thankful for the same. Had he really recognized her, or was he looking at the rusted park boundary behind her.

She expected him to come and say, "Are you...?" But no, he didn't. Proud as always, she thought. But she had her own self-respect. After living seventy years with honor, she was not so desperate to go to him herself.

She waited for some time. Then she stood up to go back. Maybe now, he would call her. She walked slowly, putting her feet on the ground blanketed with fallen leaves carefully, lest the sound of dry creaking leaves might drown a voice. The voice which she had hoped to hear fifty-four years ago, to hear now and she even wished to hear it echoing many years from now inside her grave.

At the same time he was wondering, "Was it her?" Because some minutes ago, he had felt presence of someone who he had loved fifty-four years ago but never confessed it. But he had no way to check it as he was blind as rock for last ten years.

Inkception Books

a drop of memory

by Pragya Vishnoi

Under the pink evening sky resembling the blush on the cheeks of a beautiful belle, Kang Joon Gi sighed. Unlike others, he had not come from Seoul to Varanasi, the spiritual capital of India, in search of inner peace. Instead he came in the hope of finding a drop of memory lost in the vast ocean of time. Joon Gi was sitting at the steps of Dashashwamegh Ghat of the Ganga river. There was still time left for the 'Ganga Aarti.' Diyas (Earthen lamps) floating on the Ganga were creating an ethereal ambience. The reflections on the golden surface of water were blurred, but his mind had already outlined a face amongst the crowd of hazy reflections. "Aurore, where are you?"

It appeared to Joon Gi as if Ganga was a mirror which was reflecting his past. Three years ago, he had come to Varanasi. Even then, he had not come to gain any spiritual experience; he was only fascinated by the exotic charm of a faraway country, India. As a young Korean, he was surprised by the diversity and festivities in India. But the thing that enchanted him the most was the 'Ganga Aarti.' For the first time in his life, he felt the presence of a supreme power, known as God, around him. It surprised him that so many people of different countries, ages and cultures converged for the Aarti. He was overwhelmed by the whole experience which was entirely new to him. He wanted to share his feelings with someone. But there was no one whom he knew there. He had come alone from Seoul as he didn't want anything else to distract him from discovering this unknown land. But then he realized that sometimes a person needs someone to be with him. Just as Joon Gi was glancing the people around him, his gaze collided with the face of a panic-stricken girl.

Curious, Joon Gi went towards that girl. "Is anything bothering you?" he asked the girl. She looked at him. He had not asked her, "How can I help you?" as he

Always and for Never

was not sure whether he would be able to help her. Instead he had asked her if anything was bothering her because he felt that although sharing grief can't eradicate the cause of sadness, yet it can definitely reduce its effect.

The girl replied in English, "I am Aurore from France. I came here with my friends. But I got separated from them in midst of the Ganga Aarti as I was too immersed in it. Now, I can't find the way back to my hotel. And the battery of my cellphone is also dead and I don't remember the phone numbers of my friends, so I can't contact them either."

As she spoke, Joon Gi could see her trembling fingers weaved into each other. He enquired in an earnest voice. "Haven't you asked any local person about the directions?"

"I have," replied Aurore, "but the streets of Varanasi are like a maze. They are so complicated. I got confused when the local person told me the way back to my hotel and now I don't remember what he had told me."

"What is the name of your hotel?" Joon Gi asked Aurore.

"Hotel Swagatam," was the reply.

Inkception Books

"Let's see if we can find it."

"Thanks, but won't it bother you?"

"I have nothing much to do at this time and moreover not helping a person who thinks about my convenience before her fear would not be a good thing."

Aurore smiled shyly and said, "Thanks. By the way... ." She stopped midway.

"What? Do you want to say something?"

"I was just curious. Are you Japanese or Chinese?"

Joon Gi smiled and said, "Neither. I am from Seoul, Korea."

Joon Gi asked some local persons about the way to Hotel Swagatam but no one was aware of any hotel by that name. Finally, a young Indian told him, "Here, Hotel Swagatam is not known by its name as it has been renamed this year itself. Earlier it used to have a different name. You should better ask about the hotel near Sankatmochan temple."

Then that young Indian called a rickshaw and asked the rickshaw-puller to take both Aurore and Joon Gi to the hotel.

As they both were sitting on the rickshaw, Joon

Always and for Never

Gi looked at Aurore's curly dark brown hair, which looked like a million brushes painting a beautiful picture on the canvas of air.

"What are you looking at?" Aurore asked Joon Gi.

"Nothing...Actually you are too silent and introverted, not like the lively French people."

"And who said that silent people are not lively?"

"Sorry", Joon Gi said as he looked at the rickshaw-puller who was busy listening a Bollywood song on his cell phone.

"No need to say sorry", Aurore said, smiling for the first time, "I too thought that you are not shy like other Koreans."

"Not all Koreans are shy. It seems that we both have to learn a lot about each other... I mean, each other's cultures", Joon Gi said, quickly correcting himself.

"My hotel has come," Aurore said, signaling the rickshaw-puller to stop. "Bonne nuit," she said.

"Bye," Joon Gi said. Although he couldn't understand the meaning of the last two words, he supposed that they meant 'bye' though actually they meant 'good night.'

Joon Gi said, "By the way, you didn't ask my

name. My name is..."

"No, don't tell me your name now," Aurore said, "Tomorrow we will see the famous places in Varanasi. Would you like to join us?"

"Ne, ddo bwayo," Joon Gi said quickly without realizing that Aurore could not understand Korean.

As Joon Gi hopped on the rickshaw again, he realized whether Aurore had understood that he agreed to go with her group. What if she mistook 'Ne' in Korean as 'No' in English? What if she wouldn't wait for him the next day thinking that he wouldn't come? Should he go back to her hotel to clarify it? But he thought that it would not be an appropriate thing to do and googled 'Some common French words' on his cell phone.

Contrary to all his fears, she waited for him.

"Annyeonghaseyo!" Aurore greeted him as he entered the reception area of Hotel Swagatam.

This means that Aurore too had searched for Korean words after we had parted, Joon Gi thought, with his heart fluttering, and greeted her back, "Bon jour!" Aurore smiled, "It is good that you have come. Here, meet my friends", then she introduced Joon Gi to her friends. But Joon Gi's eyes were fixed only on the sparkling eyes and

Always and for Never

sweet smile of Aurore.

That day, they roamed in the streets of Varanasi, visiting temples and places of historical importance. Aurore wanted to take a guide with them as she wanted to know every detail about the ancient city but Joon Gi was against it as he believed that the culture of a place should be experienced without any presupposition. Finally they took a guide with them, but Joon Gi never let the guide told anything before himself telling his version of things.

"What are you drinking?" Aurore asked Joon Gi when she saw him, sitting on a wooden bench of a street shop, drinking tea in a glass tumbler.

"It's tea."

"Yes, I have heard that Koreans love drinking tea."

"But this is not Korean tea," Joon Gi replied, "Every country's tea is different. Even in India, you will find different types of tea. This one is 'Masala Chai.'"

"Masala Chai? Is it tasty?"

"Very tasty... Should I order it for you?" Joon Gi said, shifting himself to other side of the bench making place for Aurore to sit on it.

Aurore nodded her head as she sat beside Joon

Gi on the bench.

Next day, when Aurore's friends went to Sarnath, she stayed back at Varanasi. Joon Gi had asked her to meet him at Dashashwamegh Ghat.

"Tomorrow I will return to Paris", Aurore said to Joon Gi, as they both were sitting on the steps of the Ghat.

"What will you do there?" Joon Gi asked Aurore, as he was gazing at the earthen lamps--diyas--floating on the river surface, in an attempt to hide his uneasiness at the thought of Aurore going back to Paris.

Aurore smiled weakly and said, "Nothing much. Perhaps I would try to rebuild my career as a painter, which has no possibility of resurrection."

"You are judging yourself too quickly," Joon Gi tried to comfort her.

"No, actually now I feel that I am not made for it. I decided to pursue painting as career because all my friends were going for it. There is something else which I want to do, which I would love to do... but what that thing is, I don't know."

"Just take it easy. Don't rush yourself into anything. Give yourself some time. If you don't find the thing

Always and for Never

you love, start loving the thing you have."

"Thanks. What do you do back in Korea?" Aurore asked. She was somewhat reassured by Joon Gi's words.

"Me? I am an Electronics engineer, work like a robot to get promotions, and when I am too burned out, I pack my bag and go for a trip", Joon Gi said in a sarcastic tone.

"Do you love your job?"

"Love is a very strong word for a job like mine. I don't love it, but I don't hate it either. It gives me money and status. And I should be grateful for it. But if I have my wish, I would rather travel the entire world, listening to the long-forgotten stories and experiencing cultures of different places."

Aurore sighed, "Let's just forget our lives in Paris and Seoul. Look at those earthen lamps floating on the Ganga. They are all different. No matter how big or small an earthen lamp is, it has to float on the river surface just like other lamps and give light. Our life is same as those lamps floating in the river of time. No matter whether we are successful or unsuccessful, happy or sad, we have to live and light the dark world with our goodness. This is the aim of our life."

Joon Gi looked into Aurore's eyes and said, "You are beautiful, Aurore".

"Thanks, and you too are not bad-looking. Especially, the hair covering your forehead look good on you", Aurore said.

"You mean that I won't look good if I have a different hairstyle?" Joon Gi asked playfully.

"I didn't mean that..."

"Okay... okay, I know that you are impressed by my good looks."

"What?"

"Just Kidding."

Aurore laughed and Joon Gi just stared at her. Then for a long time, no one spoke. Finally, Joon Gi said, "Today is your last day in Varanasi, Aurore. Don't you want to know my name now?"

"No, let our meeting remain incomplete," Aurore said in a barely audible voice.

After the Ganga Aarti, Aurore and Joon Gi together floated an earthen lamp on the Ganga river. The lamp floated towards infinity, finally disappearing in darkness.

Always and for Never

Aurore stood up to go back.

"Aurore!" Joon Gi called her from behind.

"What happened?" Aurore asked.

"Here, take it," saying this Joon Gi handed her a piece of paper with something in Devnagri script written on it.

"What's this?" Aurore asked.

"Read it later," Joon Gi said.

"I too have something for you," Aurore said, taking a wooden box out of her bag, "Open this box in Seoul after three years. I too will read your paper after three years.

After three years, when Joon Gi opened the wooden box, it was empty. He was surprised. He tried to search for the hidden unknown souvenir, but met with no success. After many days, a carving on the inner surface of the box lid caught his attention. It was something written in Devnagri script. He could not understand it. When he searched the Internet, he found out what was that carving. It was 'Sarang hae yo' in Devnagri.

Sitting on the steps of Dashashwamegh Ghat three years after his first visit for Varanasi, Joon Gi smiled, remembering what he had written in that piece of paper three years ago. He had written 'J'aime tu' in Devnagri. Now it didn't matter to him, whether Aurore read it or not. Now he was not bothered whether Aurore even remembered that she had met a Korean boy in Varanasi three years before. He was simply grateful to God that he possessed that innocent memory, which no matter how much time passed, will remain unchanged.

goodbye

by Anusha VR

He was running towards the rubble to see if anything or anyone could be salvaged from the destruction wreaked by the air strike. The air was thick with dust and smoke. But his eyes landed on a tiny glint amidst the rubble. He slowed down to locate its source. It was ring on a bloodied hand. He put all his strength in clearing the fragments of concrete and brick. He prayed that the hand way still attached to a person. A living person.

But his mind kept going back to that insignificant ring. It looked so familiar. Why did it look so familiar?

~

Inkception Books

It was the last day of summer vacation. They were sitting at Joe's Ice-cream palace. He knew she had something important to say since this was were they always came when they had big news to share. When she scored straight A's which had been every year since first grade or when he won any sporting event at school.

Halfway through their chocolate sundaes he pushed a thick plain metal ring across the table towards her.

"It's nothing. I saw it at the store the other day. Thought you would like it."

It was the ugliest ring she had ever seen.

"It is beautiful." she said and slipped it on her finger.

"So, what are we celebrating today?" he asked, trying to seem nonchalant about the ring.

"Last day of summer is reason enough, don't you think?" she said with a smile.

He nodded, his mouth too full with ice cream to formulate words. He was just happy she had worn the ring though he didn't say it out loud.

The next day at school, after Calculus she told him her family was moving.

Always and for Never

All he could register was that she was moving thousands of miles away. He tuned out everything else she said about her father and some rotten NGO. He walked away. He made every conscious effort to avoid her at school for the next week. He knew she wouldn't try and talk to him. If anyone could be more adamant than him, it was her.

She went away a week later. He never got a chance to say goodbye.

~

That was thirteen years ago when they were still in high school. Today he was kneeling on the ground hoping against all odds that that bloodied hand was connected to a body with a beating heart. When he finally cleared away the debris he saw her unblinking hazel brown eyes stare up at the cloudless blue sky. He never got a chance to say goodbye. Again.

Two more days and his tour of duty would end. Two more days and he would be back home with his wife. But none of it mattered anymore.

He was sixteen again holding the hand of the girl

he loved. He sat under the gaze of the blazing Afghan sun, holding the hand of the woman he would always love.

About the Author

Kay Elam

Kay Elam has published multiple short stories in a variety of genres with several included in The New Frontier and The Creepy Collection. When not cleaning out closets or alphabetizing her spices, she works on her elusive novel. From time to time she blogs at www.kayelam.com. She may be followed on Twitter ay kayelamwrites. A member of Mystery Writers of America and Sisters in Crime, she lives in Nolensville, TN with her husband, Greg. They are the proud grandparents of two grandsons (ages 2 and 5) and a 1-year-old granddaughter. Life is good!

Anusha VR

Anusha VR is a CA, CS, author and spoken word poet residing in India. She has performed her spoken word pieces at various venues in Kuala Lumpur and Bangalore. Her work has been published in over thirty anthologies across the world. Potpourri (Chapeltown Books UK, 2018) is her debut chapbook. She is currently working on a children's picture book.

Jennifer Steen

Jennifer Steen has written in a variety of genres and formats and plans to complete her first Science Fiction Novel soon which will be the start of a new series. She has published several other shorts professionally including: (Rain Plays Barefoot, 2011) (A Little Push, 2011) (Black Friday, 2012) (Ticker Tock, 2013). Her dramatic work (The Ghost of Twin Oaks, 2013) was selected as one of ten American high school plays to be performed in the 2013 Fringe Festival in Edinburg, Scotland. She was chosen to be a team writer for *Sleepless*, a student film production at the University of London. She continues to grow her businesses and would love to produce one of her short film scripts in the near future.

Thank You!

For more information about *Inkception Books* (book trailers, submissions, job postings, products, book signings, release parties and more) visit www.inkceptionbooks.net.

Made in the USA
San Bernardino, CA
09 February 2018